THE MARTIAN WAVE
2015

Edited by J Alan Erwine

THE MARTIAN WAVE 2015
A science fiction magazine
Edited by J Alan Erwine

Cover: Mars
Cover design by Laura Givens

First printing August 2015

Nomadic Delirium Press
Aurora, Colorado
http://www.nomadicdeliriumpress.com

Table of Contents
Stories

Poems

From An Unnamed Rock
By Jerry L. Robinette

Wriggling into the suit like a caterpillar into its cocoon, right foot first then the hand, drop the shoulder, step in and squeeze, left elbow tight against my ribs and hand on my thigh, then the hand slides up and by twisting the arm a little the elbow slips in and the left hand is in. Now point the toe and hyperextend the knee a bit, never thought I'd be glad for those Yoga classes with what's-her-name, the redhead with the incredible ass and her hair smelling of lavender, at least I got something out of all that stretching--Marcella, that was it, now clap hands and bring the gauntlets together and the front seam interlocks and seals with a hiss so I nod at the camera and Doug Frantz (who thinks he's the King of Cool but is really just Captain Corporate) flips a switch and the helmet lowers--damn, I'm using that ear! At least it clicked into place OK, now keep my nose clear while it rotates, sealing me in with the delicate aromas of disinfectant and insulating foam over the baseline reek of my own sweat, display says I'm still alive and everything's green, never noticed how bright those indicators are, somebody should put some work into the aesthetics of the Command Module. Wonder how many of 'em would turn amber if I held my breath a while, hold it long enough and I could get some of them to red, bet that'd make ol' Dougie Boy warp out, but then I'd get my hands slapped for sure, gotta be a company reg of some kind about that.

"Looks good on this end, Ron. You're green three by six, pressures within tolerances. Confirm comms and internal status, and your chariot awaits."

Yeah, I'll give you a call if I can't hear you, ya meathead, but that's what the guidebook says to ask, right, and who knows, maybe do a little song and dance unless it violates regs about keeping this as dull and irritating as possible.

"Comm confirmed and working. Internal status is green two by three. Ready for insertion, Captain."

"Roger. Initializing transfer and preparing for separation, but if you're not sure about doing this, Ron, now is the time to say so. I can land you remotely from here and make life easier for all of us."

"Thanks for the offer, I guess. I'd just as soon do this myself." If I were any other miner would you make that offer, or are you just being patronizing because you think I'm still crying over Kelli?

"Roger that, it's your call."

He started to say "my funeral" but realized at the last minute that would be frowned upon by the bean counters who sign our paychecks, or maybe he's sure I'll take a tumble and he'd feel like it was his fault, like he pre-ordained it for me, delusions of grandeur. Ah, I love the feel of the vibration of the servos coming up through the boots of the Excursion Suit, but no feeling of motion as I'm trundled into the Lander, feels like I'm inside a cannon shell, once more into the breech, but not much firepower in my little popgun Lander; more of a shelving unit for me and the gear, the minimum for dropping to the rock, planting the factory and--physics and Cap'n Doug willing--getting back in the CM; I'm not really a Lander Pilot or geologist, hell not even a real miner, truth be told, just a guy delivering a box to a dusty potato, some carbonaceous hunk of leftover crud from the formation of the solar system, doesn't even deserve a name, Near Earth Asteroid Something-Something-Something-Five, I'm pretty sure the last one was a five, or maybe a nine. Either way, this ain't Luna, none of Aldrin's "magnificent desolation," no craggy mountains or sprawling seas of regolith, just a couple of flat spots and a few kilotons of mine-able ice, and I might as well be delivering a pizza. OK, if this hasn't locked into place yet--there we go, that feels right.

"Fledgling this is Mother Hen. I show transfer complete and control systems linked. Please confirm."

Yeah, now that I'm safe and sound in my rickety-assed LM we get all formal, almost like you know when they're gonna start recording radio traffic for playback in the media. Statuses green here, too, let's see if the thrusters are working, for what they're worth . . .just a flick, Ronnie, light touch, lighttouch. OK on X plus and minus, now Y, two for two, now the Z, flick and flick, good, this'll make him so happy, wouldn't want to ruin his big separation speech, and still solid green across the board, nuthin' could be finer--

"Switching video to landing mode, Fledgling. Please confirm."

"Roger that Mother Hen, video confirmed, looks like we're open for business. Thrusters all test positive and all indicators green on this end."

Carbonaceous crud, leftover building blocks. . .

"Synced with target at one point six kilometers, point oh two crossrange, two minutes from separation on your mark, Fledgling."

. . . potato-shaped lump of dirt and dust, in ultra-high contrast in the video screen on the inner bulkhead, no color and almost no texture but exotic all the same, alien soil for all its lifelessness....

"Mother Hen this is Fledgling, confirming all systems go, commence separation procedure . . . mark."

That's the only techno-chatter sound-bite you'll get from me, Cap'n, no more time for that crap as my little LM rotates two degrees and breaks connections with the Command Module, then a blazing swath of pinprick stars slides left as I remain static relative to my video screen, again no sense of motion but that shudder is the CM edging away, leaving me in the potato's micro-gravity.

"Decoupling complete. You are go for the first manned landing on Near Earth Asteroid 31665 and establishment of the newest extra-terrestrial mining facility, another small stepping-stone in mankind's expansion from the cradle of Mother Earth. God speed, Fledgling!"

Barf! Get some new writers, Cap'n, now excuse me while I do this, this is about where Kelli was when she lost it, too focused on her rate of descent and lost sight of her crossrange, rolled the lander and died before it came back upright, Excursion Suits can only cushion so much. But I'm sweeter than Momma's lemonade, descent is perfect and almost straight down, so at least he cut me loose clean. Got to zoom out on the video, that's a big crater but I'll miss it easy, rest of it looks flat as a plate of piss, fine by me. Uh-oh, drifting a little, here we go, light touch, lighttouch, lightlight--sweet, OK, don't over-correct now, there we go.

"Fledgling we show you at 100 meters and green for landing."

Yeah, no shit, now shut up and let me do this, 75 meters and Jeezus, where'd my video go, what--oh, dust cloud, last burst must've hit a pile of the stuff, great, now I can barely see--50 meters, slow down, Ronnie, you got this, nice and easy--

"Quite a dust plume, Fledgling. You might want to hover for a minute to let it clear so you can visually confirm your landing site is still a go."

Helluva idea, if I had clear video, Cap'n, 30 meters, rate of descent good, a bit of drift but fixable with a quick flick of the ol' joystick, there we go. Hey, that cleared my video and it looks OK, some shiny patches now, ice would be my guess, 20 meters and as light as a feather, gentle, gentle, just a touch of thrust, one last look down, and, and, and here.

"Fledgling to Mother Hen, we are down, solid, green across the board. How's my telemetry?"

"Congratulations, Fledgling. You look great from up here; set your anchors and you are go for excursion."

Dust still settling, the whole LM vibrates as the augers screw into the crust of my little interplanetary roadside rest, hope they anchor this baby good since we have no gravity to speak of, rotation alone could almost send me spinning off and that would suck. Bite deep, my little friends, we've made it this far so let's get the job done and get back, I ain't going anywhere for a few minutes, so I guess now's a good time to see if I can remember the set-up sequence for the mining unit, the CM could walk me through it but let's just try to do it our own self, shall we, just to earn our paycheck, OK?

"Mother Hen to Fledgling, nice landing, Ron. That dust plume had me shaking a little, but you're within 15 meters of target, and that's a damned fine landing. Switching all systems to survey mode."

He sounds different, must've cut out the broadband FM so nobody can hear us but us, who wants to listen to this stuff anyway, just the wheels of industry turning, grinding away, making a few bucks for the bossman by pulling water from the rocks and ain't that a hoot.

"Thanks, couldn't have done it without ya. Survey mode confirmed."

Watch the little screen and see the camera pan as I nudge the joystick, just a little puddle of gray light as we rotate through the darkness here, the vibration has stopped and all four augers show secure, time to get out of this flying outhouse and get my boots dirty, regolithy, whatever.

"Mother Hen to Fledgling, we show you anchored and all indicators green for EVA. You might want to take a minute after you step out and have a look due east before you get too

busy."

"Roger, Mother Hen."

"East" just means in the direction of my rock's rotation, since we have nothing like magnetic north. Flip the lever to release the pneumatic clamps holding my Excursion Suit to the LM, that cough as they release still reminds me of the old man there toward the end, now to climb down without breaking my neck, like playing on the jungle gym in mid-winter, all coats and gloves but just scary enough to be fun.

OK, now down and, there we go, a few footprints, but nobody to take pictures of 'em, like posterity gives a damn, nothing historic here, just us working stiffs. . . ya load 16 tons and whaddaya get, something, something, something and deeper in debt . . . now what was Mother Hen talking about, due East? Holy crap, look at that! Never pictured it that big, reflecting so much light, this whole rock swimming in pale blue Earth-glow and it's just ... wow. So that's what it is, what we all are, together on that balloon, twirling through space-time.

"Thanks for the tip Mother Hen. That's a nice show you arranged."

"Can't take credit for that one, Fledgling, but glad you enjoyed it. Now get to work, you've got four hours left down there."

"Roger, Mother Hen."

*

That should hold for a few decades and I've got what, one-point-four hours left, great, plenty of time to catch my breath before climbing back in, can double-check those power couplings to the solar array while I catch my breath and wait for Mother Hen to run the diagnostics, speaking of Captain Corporate he should be coming up--yeah, there he is, sailing over my southern horizon, some ancient deity riding his parabolic steed across the heavens, and there he goes, doesn't take long up here, yeah those connections look tight, the number three strut isn't anchored as tight as I would like, but it's within tolerances, so screw it . . . .

"Fledgling to Mother Hen, installation complete and final checks show positive. Initiate external diagnostics at will, I'll wait for your confirmation before locking in."

"Copy that, Fledgling. Initiating remote diagnostic sequence now. You may as well climb back into place, these never really find anything."

Let's not get in a hurry, Ron, remember, baby steps, I'm the only thing not really anchored down right now, hey, look, I can do a chin-up, wearing three hundred pounds of gear! Ya put your left boot in, ya put your right boot in, then ya lock those suckers down . . . .

"Mother Hen here. Diagnostics all come back fine on the mining unit, and you're still green across the board. Advise when you're ready to initiate return sequence. Well done, Ron."

"Roger Mother Hen. And thanks."

*

What the Hell? How--how, slow down, Ron, deep slow breath, get some oxygen, try to think, what, oh, yeah, shit, I hit the switch for main thrust and. . . slow down, check your displays, still have air so I'm not leaking anywhere, hands and feet are working and it doesn't-- yeowtch, that hurts like a sumbitch, gotta be a busted collarbone or dislocated shoulder or something.

"Mother Hen to Fledgling, please acknowledge. Mother Hen to Fledgling, please acknowledge."

"Fledgling here, or what's left of it."

"What's your condition, Fledgling?"

"I'm OK I think, except for a banged-up shoulder, but, what the Hell happened?"

"When you applied thrust the LM tilted and then rolled. As best I can make out from the video, one of your struts never retracted its auger. That was ten minutes ago."

"Copy that, Mother Hen. I still have air and the suit appears to have maintained its integrity"--or I'd be just another piece of debris by now— *"haven't checked LM integrity yet."*

"We've got you on video, Ron. At least one leg of the LM appears badly damaged. Are you able to try to climb out of the damned thing? Telemetry says thruster fuel pressure is dropping and we can't tell where it's going. But go easy, it may not be stable."

"Roger all that."

Nothing wants to move, damned pneumatic clamps didn't let go, switch is--damn, gotta take it easy on that side!--there we go, now try to figure out which end is up, can't see the video screen so have to work by feel, and I can't feel shit through this suit, who suggested putting us in these freaking tin cans anyway, there we go, now if that foot will come clear of whatever is . . . OK, good, there's the control panel so the hatch must be . . . ah, screw the hatch just go out between the struts, easyonthatshoulder and step down. Ta-da. Take that, you over-priced piece of government-built garbage!

"Fledgling to Mother Hen, I'm clear of the LM."

Yikes, been a long time since I got a headache like that just from standing up, musta taken a real good knock on the melon. No sign of the leak, yeah that right front leg never did let go, still anchored to the ground, I wonder . . . maybe landed on ice, the friction from the auger going in melted it, and when it refroze it gummed up the works, that's my guess, man, that leg took some serious torque, looks like the world's worst greenstick fracture. What's that in the--oh, just Mother Hen coming up again, moving faster now, probably tightened his orbit to get visual on me.

"Mother Hen here, Ron. How are you feeling? And have you had a chance to look the situation over?"

"Affirmative on the eval, feeling OK, still a little buzzing in my ears and my left shoulder is sub-optimal right now, possible broken collarbone. I'm trying to think how I'm going to get out of here and mostly coming up with answers that don't work, so far. What's your view?"

"Options appear somewhat limited; Fledgling is grounded until the company can get a team up here with replacement parts. And the Command Module doesn't have the superstructure to land on anything, let alone take off. "

"You telling me I have to walk home?"

"I'm saying we don't yet know the best way of getting you off there. Walking may not be totally unrealistic."

"Really? So you're thinking . . . I'm under a fraction of one percent of Earth gravity. If I were a rock, I could throw myself into orbit and off of my little island paradise. Problem is, once I get my feet off the ground, all I'll have for control is two minutes of the compressed-air jets in this suit. Maybe less if they've been leaking or got triggered in the fall. So you'll have to catch me. "

Don't just keep going around like that, say something. Unless you've got a better plan this has to work, or I'll just mark off a prime piece of real estate for the cemetery and start digging my own grave, that would ruin the property values, but who would want to build a condo next to an automated ice-mine anyway? There's one born every minute, I guess, and with Kelli already gone the kids could use the income from my real estate empire, but they wouldn't get much--

"Sorry to go quiet on you Ron, just reading the results of the latest simulation, and this should work fine. Basically, once you're off the rock, we just plot your trajectory, transition to a matching orbit, and rendezvous. Pretty much exactly as

14

planned, except you leave the lander there."

"Sounds good. And what did the computer say are the chances of it working?"

"Probability of success is pretty high, better odds than you get on some commercial flights these days."

Either he couldn't do the calculation or he knows I won't like the answer and either way does not inspire confidence.

"Sure, sounds plausible enough. What's first on the new checklist?"

Of course there's a new checklist, because he wouldn't commit to anything like this without signoff from control and they wouldn't sign off on anything that didn't have a checklist.

"Practice hopping for a few minutes to get a feel for it, then go to your southern horizon, take a couple of giant steps and use the top of the lander for one last bounce, then you need about 10 seconds of maximum thrust straight up with your suit jets. That puts you well past escape velocity. It will take us a few minutes to crunch the numbers and set up our transition, and then we swing by and pick you up."

"I gotta give you points for creativity, Doug. You must be one of them rocket scientists."

"Just a humble engineer, trying to earn a semi-honest buck. The only potential snags are you smacking into us on your way out--I will stand a little clear to prevent that--or you not having the air in the suit jets to do some necessary maneuvering for the rendezvous, in which case I may have to come out and get you."

"Who am I to argue with a humble engineer? I only have one question before we start."

"What's that, Ron?"

"Where do you think we should build the shopping mall?"

"Uh, Ron, you're not running short of air or anything, right? Your telemetry still looks good--"

"Forget it, Doug. Just doing a little long-range planning for

15

the subdivision I'm going to build up here."

"Fair enough, tell me all about it when you get back, maybe I'll invest in it with you. Now, start small with the practice hops, you don't want to use your suit jets unless you have to. And wait for my 'Go' before you make the big jump. Clear?"

"Roger, wilco, Doug. Hopping away toward the south horizon now."

Baby steps, Ron, baby steps 'cause I can't afford to screw this up, this is definitely a one-shot deal, but at least the mechanics are simple enough, and that's more of a chance than she had . . . whoa! It's not the distance so much as the waiting to come down part that feels freaky, the body has to adjust to the timing, OK, better, still not great, and that landing was not as soft as I had hoped, gotta use the pain to stay awake, to keep focused. Wish I could run but that's out of the question in this damned suit. Guess I should be more respectful, it's saved my life so far, that felt better, gotta keep my legs from trying to rotate out from under me now. I bet surfing is something like this, only faster. And with more water. So, maybe surfing is nothing like this at all--PAY ATTENTION, damnit, you're gonna screw around and get yourself dead. Christ, landings are hard on a bunged up shoulder even in micro gravity, I'm going to take every freakin' pain-killer in the med-kit when I get back aboard the Mother Hen, I swear to God. Hey, nice one, I may be getting the hang of this.

"It's about that time, Ron. You think you're ready?"

"Roger, Mother Hen. Pour me a scotch, no rocks--ha ha-- and set out a few aspirin. I'm ready to come home."

"How sure are you that you can hit the top of the lander for your bounce point, Ron?"

"Willing to bet my life on it, Doug. Seriously, I'm as ready as I'm gonna get."

"Roger that, friend. And you're in the right position, so on *my mark . . . Go!"*

Smooth and easy, Ron, smooth and easy, four hops to the lander there's one, whoops, a little wobble, nothing to panic about, keep those legs under ya, there's two, still on line, range looks right. Need a little more height in three to get the angles to work out, and . . . . OK, here we go it's lined up, now I just need to stick the lander--gotta remember that line when I get back!--and YES! Now jump hard man, jump and then the suit jets, woo-hoo, they got juice! One-Mississippi, two-Mississippi, three-Mississippi, how gorgeous, a little Earth-shine, for my going away party, maybe Kel got to see that before she died . . . how many Mississippi, screw it, I'm clear, may as well save my jets for the link-up and just enjoy the view. Look at all the stars, so many stars and I'll probably never get to visit half of 'em. But at least I've made it this far. And here comes my ride.

Rip van Winkle on Mars
By David C Kopaska-Merkel

I'd dreamed a Martian tundra:
tussocks, tiny flowers--
I guess I overslept

Dome open to the thin cold sky,
rooms agape, no thing left behind,
a burn mark where the lander crouched
is their goodbye

out back a midden: wrappers, boxes;
hunkering, I see a bit of gray-green mold
inside a plastic wrap,
company is good, but for companionship
I'll need to wait a few billion years.

I *could* use a nap.

On the Bridge
By Matthew Spence

Castillo leaned into the wind, his powered suit aiming the fusing beam in between the unhealed cracks, seeing them repair themselves as the beam stitched the meta-material together. When he was done, Castillo told the suit's rigging line to take him back up to the span. Looking to his left, he saw other workers doing the same, and was thankful that this part of the bridge was finally ready for rail and slab sections to be laid in.

Castillo greeted the rest of the crew as he went to the Boss Booth to sign out of his shift. The Boss 'bot accepted his report, recognizing that Castillo and the others would be compensated with credit bits for the extra work. The loading platform's safety field crackled electric blue as it let Castillo and his crew into the habitat shuttle. The shuttle had been their home for more than a year since the job started, having followed the Bridge's progress from one hemisphere of this world to another. It was an ambitious project, begun before Castillo and his crew had arrived from Earth, built by a combination of human and robot labor that worked under the planet's water-filled clouds. Various contractors had bid for the work, and the rapid progress meant that somebody back home was making a lot of money. Castillo liked to think he helped make that happen, and hoped that he would be present at the end when the Bridge was officially dedicated, but that probably wouldn't happen. He was the equivalent of a migrant worker, a temporary hired hand, and would go on to other projects, most likely orbital habitats circling some Super Earth. But at least he'd know what he'd done.

Castillo had a drink in the shuttle's bar as it tracked back up the span. There was a group of new workers in, kids half his age who were straight out of the Engineering Academy. They talked about stuff that didn't interest him; mainly local impact studies and how they might affect their jobs. That told him they were locals, and as such he and the other workers tended to keep some distance between them. Migrants weren't popular on some worlds, although so far that hadn't been the case here, where everybody was from somewhere else.

One of them, a kid named Pike that Castillo knew slightly, sat down next to him. Castillo had seen him on the standby crew from time to time. "So," Pike casually said, "Have you heard the strike talk that's been going around lately?"

Castillo frowned. He didn't like mixing politics and work. "I suppose everybody has," he cautiously replied. "Why are you so interested? Thinking of staging an occupation?"

He'd meant it as a joke, but the kid suddenly looked apprehensive, perhaps even excited.

"It's on," he said, lowering his voice as if he was afraid somebody might be listening.

Castillo shook his head. "I wouldn't listen to rumors if I were you. If there was a strike coming, there'd be union announcements, postings on their site, and Management would be here, with security drones. Besides, we've crossed the hemisphere; we'll be connecting with the other half of the Bridge inside of a year at most. Why stage a strike at this late date?"

"Some of the workers I've been talking to say it's a statement-they want Earth to know who built the Bridge, that it wasn't an investor's group from the EU, the Eurasian Union or the Americas. They..."

"You don't look old enough to have even been to Earth yet," Castillo reminded him. "Look, you hear these things sometimes when a job is almost finished. On another world they might even be true, but here, where everybody's bidding for the same amount of bits and a homeworld contract? When is this supposed to take place, anyway?"

"During the Bridge's anniversary, when the Territorial Governor makes her speech." The kid suddenly looked more nervous; which made Castillo wonder if there was something to this after all. "Look, I don't want to get into trouble. I'm a contract worker; I don't believe in violence."

"No problem." Castillo saw Pike breathe a sigh of relief as he nodded and hurried away. Castillo was no snitch, but he'd heard about some of these groups that were opposed to the Bridge, mainly for environmental reasons. But even the Greens back home actually supported the Bridge, with its maglev trains, as an alternative to ground traffic. The only people who would really be opposed, he reasoned, would be other investors who lost their bids for contracts...

Castillo sat at the bar, thinking about the cracks he'd seen in the support pillars. They'd been happening more frequently lately. Sure, he got more bits repairing them, but it also slowed down the work, which cost more to finish in the long run...

Castillo heard the first explosion as it shook the Bridge, causing the entire span to rock back and forth before it thankfully settled. He was surprised that the detectors hadn't gone off, when a second, smaller explosion followed. Castillo joined the other workers, including Pike, as they streamed out of the shuttle, where they could see blue and white smoke coming from the span they'd just been working on. Pike looked just as shocked as the rest of them.

Castillo didn't see Pike again for the next week or so, during which time repair teams and investigators went over the damage. They didn't release their findings right away, but the crews were allowed to go back to work by the end of the week, under the watchful eye of an autonomous drone that circled overhead.

Pike reappeared in the bar the following weekend. "You

were right," he said. "They'd been planning this for weeks, even months. I didn't want to believe they'd actually go through with it, but they were committed. And it was about money, after all. Somebody back home wanted a contract, and didn't get it, so they sabotaged the metamaterials to weaken them, so that their own crews could repair them. But they didn't figure on the fusing beams being able to heal them so quickly. That's when they decided on the bombs. They were going to make it look like an accident, but got caught. The people who actually planned this all lived back on Earth; they've never even been here."

"Well, they're being prosecuted for it now," Castillo said. "You shouldn't blame yourself."

Pike nodded, but then he looked down at the bar. "But I should have done something," he said, suddenly sounding much older than his years. He got up and slowly walked out of the bar, shaking his head. Castillo watched him leave with sympathy.

He never came back.

Mars Ride Along
By EJ Shumak

I wake and have no idea where I am. I always wake to confusion. They said we would get used to the environment. That was as much crap as everything else about this mission.

"Мне все равно", Great. It was the Russians arguing again that woke me. Well I suppose it's better than sleeping and dreaming. This last time I woke up thinking there was still a NASA and the US led the world in the solar system. I guess my dreams are even older than I am.

I didn't want anything to do with the Russians; I don't understand why they were even on this mission. Granted we needed the Japanese, or we weren't getting anywhere. Wow, I really am arrogant, Like WE need the Japanese, Hell yeah; problem is they don't need us. Kinda neat all I have to do is change "us" to "US" and I go from personal to prewar political. If I thought us/US was arrogant, the Russians give the team nothing but arrogance and grief.

They couldn't even get along together; one of them claimed to be Ukrainian, even though there was no Ukraine. I didn't even know how or why that happened. First there was a Ukraine, then there wasn't, then there was again, then us/US got involved and all hell broke loose.

They taught us that no one believed Putin was crazy enough to loose his nukes -- destroyed nearly a quarter of Earth, The orders to launch are obeyed and then, just two weeks later, Putin is slaughtered by his own cabinet. I definitely don't understand Russians. The Ukrainians no longer had a country and us/US was just a shade better than third world.

Now I'm headin' for Mars with Russians under Nihon command and we speak American English. Three more months, and personally I don't believe there is a station there anymore. I got no use for Japanese command either. I still believe in American superiority, only a memory now.

"Duerr, I need the Davidavich relieved."

"Right, Lieutenant Commander." I get two points for that one. I didn't call him Captain, but referred to his rank, Sato hated that but couldn't bring himself to complain because I was still accurate as to rank if not command status. I also didn't mention his "the Davidavich" slip. But Daichi knew he messed up. He always knew. I couldn't wait to tell Yasue. She'd make him feel even more worthless than I could. I smiled.

Kicking off my bunk rail, I sailed through the comm station up to navigation. I slammed into Davidavich, using the back of his crash couch for a brake.

"пошел на хуй"

"Hey be nice comrade, I'm here to relieve you, not just wake you up. Watch the language too pal, we don't have a problem now, but I'm open if you are." He just glared at me, unbuckled and pushed off back down the core. Again, I smiled. It seemed to be my only defense, my only pleasure and my only option.

My buddy Davidavich left shift after doing absolutely nothing. No tracings, no positioning, hell we could be headed for Venus instead of Mars for all that lazy shit knew. I scrunched down into the cushions, trying to give myself an illusion of gravity or at least G-force by jerkin' the crash straps tight.

We had so little to do on this mission, I'm amazed anybody could avoid work. I was happy as a clam in dogshit to have something to take my mind off home. Not to mention why I volunteered for a multi-year mission that I believed was at best a waste and at worst a suicide run. Just enough of my mind is absorbed into these calculations and sensor checks to allow myself to really think.

Maybe I can figure out what the damn dreams mean. Not the regular ones, not the ones about me still being with Sharon. I just can't shake those memories, not even this far away. I thought I could escape, but no, I just get these new even weirder dreams, just as we passed through the mars belt. A hallucination or two if I admit it.

I'm falling and there's a hand, no a tentacle no – I just can't focus on it. Where the hell? I pop back into the navcomp, just like I never left. Crap. I was just gone forty-five minutes arguing with some something that wanted to pull me up and save me. Yeah right – save me I'm sure.

Mindless important crap has always been the way I can turn inward and look at my life. When I was a kid I used handload ammunition to zone out. If I made a mistake, I was likely to blow myself up. That kept the analytic part of my mind busy, while my emotional mind went nuts (almost literally) with the freedom to consider everything. And I'm still here. Our progressive government no longer allows such socially evil activities, so handloading would be out even if I was home. But they still let me sit console and run numbers, simulations, and cross checks. Kinda' the same thing, 'cept I can't step outside for some air, or lack thereof. And I'm not so good at avoiding these visits from my tentacle friends.

Nine hours go by and I'm just caught up. I wonder if I'm the only one who actually does the Nav work. I actually had Davidavich tell me "Я не делаю математику" (I don't do math) or close. The Russian is just simple enough that I can make most of it out. I acted like I didn't understand. I don't want the commies to think I can translate their insults. The vicious profane insults. Even they figure stuff like that transcends language barriers.

Lieutenant JG Ishikawa is scooting down the Core towards my station. I smell her long before I can see or hear her. This recycled air is another gift of our need to survive out here where we probably don't belong. But, unlike the cabbage smelling Boris crew, Yasue's olfactory announced presence is more than welcome.

"Have a good rest with computer games, Captain?"

This is rich. I'm a senior tech with the nominal rank of Captain, IE I wear railroad tracks on the uniform, but the Nihon Navy calls that a Lieutenant, 'course us/US did/does too. The Captain's sled is calling me Captain. "Yasue, it is always a pleasure to see you. Games are all finished now. Hey, you gonna' relieve me?"

"Unfortunately, no. You must remember I have essential science duties to perform. I am only here as messenger. Perhaps we will someday develop another means of more efficient communication, oops –well"

"Ok I know you are much more important member of this mission, but I can still get us all real lost, real quick. Don't think that the Borises can save you."

"Though you terrify me, I will still tell you of your good fortune. You have been bestowed the privilege of monitoring the other Greg on a repair excursion at the core base."

"When?"

"You have only thirty minutes to contemplate your great fortune. 2240 at the aft deck plate."

"You are stunningly beautiful even when you are mean." And she was. Too bad the real Captain was riding that sled.

"I accept the compliment and ignore the insult. I am genetically incapable of being mean. It is in my culture, Sempai."

"Who's my relief?"

"Abe."

"And where is Ensign Abe?"

"Just behind me. Fear not, you will not be late for your

repair work. Unless I cannot trust you alone with her."

"Again, you wound me Lieutenant." She smiled and kicked hard off the back of my crash couch. "You're gonna' hurt yourself one day Yasue." At least Ensign Abe wasn't doubling up with anyone in the sleep tubes. At least that I could determine. She did take another five minutes to show up though.

"I've got your back, Lieutenant. I hope you left me with something to do."

"Not for another hour or so, when new scans are complete." Her name, Hitome suited her. She did have beautiful eyes. Damn, I have to keep that part of my brain in check. "I'll transfer to you now, if you don't mind. I have repair monitor duty in about twenty minutes, aft. And please call me Greg."

"That is difficult for me, Sempai. I do not know you so well. Besides, how could I tell you from Ensign Carlson?"

I smiled, "True, we are so much alike. Heck we're both Americans." All I got back was a return smile and those sparkling eyes. I grabbed the core rail and shoved myself aft towards the lockers to tool up. Hell, from here everything was aft.

*

Carlson was waiting for me when I got to the aft access panel. "Greg"

"Greg"

"Sorry if I'm late."

"I don't think it's anything anyway. Our fearless leader has been acting even weirder than normal lately. Don't tell me you didn't notice. You two being so close. You being his first officer and all."

"Honestly I didn't. He's so damn creepy anyway. I just keep tryin' to irritate him and stay out of actionable shit." *Wow, did the only other American on board think I was tight with Somber Sato?* "Ya know Ensign, my friend; He has never given me any reason to suspect that I am first officer. I think he would have to die for the Borises to realize it."

"Well I know who should have been commanding this mission."

"Hell, is your nose brown – what do you know that I don't?"

"I know I am having the weirdest and most disturbing dreams of my life. I know you're having them too because the screams I hear are in clear US English."

"Hell, I'm screaming in my damn sleep?"

"Yes, Sir. And the screams are freaking me out." Nobody else bitched about it? Maybe they think it's all me."

"Anyway, what are we lookin' for?"

"The Captain says there is leakage in the thermo-couplings that cross water recycling and heat."

"And he knows this how?"

"I don't ask. That's the first officer's job."

"Thanks. OK get down in the tunnel. Ya know I'm too damn fat to get in there."

"Hey, just because you're "Big Greg" doesn't mean I should suffer."

"No, you're right. That is unfair – wait, you suffer because you are both a Tech and an Ensign."

"OK OK , I'm crawling boss."

As I lean against the bulkhead, I start to remember stuff. Thoughts that are somehow commands, and I reject them. As if I know they're just plain wrong – and too damn weird too. Were those dreams? Was I screaming? Hell if I know. But the Russians and Sato have been subdued lately. Even Davidavich let my threat go unanswered this afternoon. I didn't think anything of it then, I guess I just thought I was a big, tough American first officer. But that would just antagonize any of the Borises even more. "What ya got, Carlson?"

"Nothing yet. No moisture visible, no moisture on the instruments, Water system is optimal as is the heat pump."

"Screw it. Get back up here. If Daichi couldn't give you specifics, then we're done."

"You call him that?"

"Hell, not to his face. Tried it with Yasue once and got slapped for my trouble. I can just imagine what Sato would do. The Borises said he has ceremonial edged weapons in his locker. I'd be the crew's fresh meat for sure. You hungry for that kinda fresh meat?"

"Not yet, sir. I'll let you know, or let Sato know."

"OK wise ass. Crawl on outta there. If you weighed anything or if I could tell up from down without a sign, I'd help ya outta there"

"I do not believe you for one second, Lieutenant."

I jammed myself into the bulkhead corner near the hatchway to stabilize myself. I still kinda freaked when I just float away. "Talk to me a bit more on these dreams."

"One Nihon is having them too. I think it's Ishikawa, based on the minimal accent and female voice."

"Anybody else? I asked."

"I don't think so. Not that I heard."

"You were born in the twenties right, after Putin?"

"Yeah, you too."

"Obviously I know that. But Ishikawa's parents were living in the US during Putin. She was born on US soil after the nukes. I think she's the only foreign US first born that survived"

"Shit"

"No damn kidding Shit. The corpsman's worthless. Don't talk to him. I'll look into it – I don't know what the hell I'm looking into or why, but I will. A lot of stuff has happened to first borns after Putin. I mean we hardly get sick and we're supposed to be a bit stronger. But that makes sense. I mean 90% of us died before birth. And we got three of the remaining four thousand here on this mission. But we're different. I never consider anything coincidental with after Putin first borns"

"Yes Sir."

"Write up your report and give it to Sato. I'll talk to ya later."

"Sir", Carlson said as I left him there cleaning up. I was headed to the only private space I had. My sleep tube. I was overdue for downtime as it was.

I slipped into my tube and keyed up main comm. Arkady had the duty, "Yes, sir Lieutenant."

"I'm off shift and down. Will notify when back on deck. Don't buzz me for less than the Captain or a class two."

"Acknowledged and logged, sir. Comm out."

I fall off right away.

Suddenly I am back in Appleton. The ground is swimming with these curved pieces of meat, at least that's what it looks like to me. Hell, it's my dream, I guess it's exactly what I say it is. The meat wigglers are much deeper now, past my knees and I'm wading through 'em. Redish, with some kind of mouth, searching and biting. I kick up as many as I can and they seem agitated, at least they are moving faster and jumping higher. There's a shelf about one quarter click forward. I run for it, or rather slosh towards it, the Reds biting at me, my legs have started to ache and I fall forward into the pool of warm red slime that surrounds me.

Suddenly I'm calm, voices, lots of voices, singing to me in soft lullaby. My Grandmother is there, beckoning me down, deeper into the red. I look at her. The one human being that completely and unconditionally loved me looks back with not grayish blue eyes, but with short tentacles pulsing and angling from the sockets. This time I know I awake screaming. I lay quietly – I do not sleep.

The last mission started having innocuous communications and reports just before they reached Mars station. One week later Mars station went silent. Timing wise, we went through the same general area of the asteroid belt that Mars Seventeen traversed. We are Mars Eighteen.

I realize now that I was completely lax in any first officer duties reasonably expected of me. I followed Sato's orders even if they were bullshit because I knew that's what he wanted. I flirted with his girlfriend and did all the Borises work and thought I was this great selfless leader. I failed to notice that the rest of the crew was just one step up from zombies. Damn I hate that word, but I don't know how else to describe it. The Russians don't even argue anymore. Everybody does the minimum. No more bitchin'. No more nothing.

I have the dreams, but they stay in the background. They definitely want control. I know I know, how the hell do I know what the dreams want – but I do know.

I pass Yasue in the core. I grab her, hard. "Look I don't know if you're still in there, but if you are get in your tube and stay there until after we dock. I'll come get you then." She glares at me, but doesn't answer. And she sure as hell doesn't slap me.

I head to the armory and punch in my override codes. I just hope Sato is too far gone to notice or realize what I'm doing. I pull out three antiquated 1911's. Damn near 150 years old, but they'll work. And a laser cutting tool. I look even fatter floating down (yeah right down) towards my sleep tube. I slip in with my collection and wait.

*

The jostling of positional jets followed by a loud clank and whirring noises inform me of all I need to know. We're docked

31

and locked. Shadows keep passing my tube. I have it tinted 85%. I can barely see anything but no one can see in. That's so much more important. I figure four minutes for the crew to clear and at least three more to figure out some of us are missing.

I pop outta my tube and key in the emergency seal code. The three sectional bulkheads slam shut and the seals reengage at the forward docking collar. No alarms like in the movies – thank heavens. All I need now are alarms.

I belt in at the helm and jerk us off station. Carlson is coming up behind me and my firing of the positioning jets slam his head against the core.

"Thanks ass hole"

"No problem, You can thank me again later. Get up here and grab a 1911. Just make sure you only hit SOFT targets. We can't hole the ship."

"Hey, I'm not an idiot just because we got the same name."

"Hopefully you won't find anyone, except maybe Yasue."

A voice echoes from further aft in the core, "I'll even let you guys call me that now. Save me one of those Colts."

*

I couldn't be happier. Well I guess I could, but under the circumstances at least it was three for home. And only 27 hours to the next communications window. I think I'll let the science expert handle that duty.

The Star Chaser
By Christina Sng

Bella perches on the edge
Of the Black Eye Galaxy,
Watching like a dark sentinel.

She's gone from hunting Leviathans
To chasing rogue stars
In the last million cycles,

Tracking the ones with the ability
To escape black holes. A fairy tale
Once told to her as a little girl.

It's a suicide mission but she's lived
Too long to care. Her drive is
Uncovering secrets, not eternal life.

This black hole is massive,
Spanning a thousand galaxies.
It is devouring stars

Like a rabid zombie.
Yet two stars slip past
Its formidable gravity.

Bella takes an enormous leap,
Following them through the dead zone.
They repel her easily, escaping

Into the void. Then she realizes
How they've eluded

The black hole's magnetic pull.

They emit and control
Repulsive antigravity,
A legendary power among stars.

No one believed they were real
Until now.
Bella can hardly believe it herself.

She can testify she's seen them,
But she knows the Elders
Will capture them, harness

Their power, and destroy them
After the torture. Bella believes
Even stars deserve their freedom,

As she stays a minute
To admire them, then leaves
To track down her next bounty:

A mysterious phasing star.

I'll Take the Moon
By Andrew L MacDonald

The stale green letters of the countdown clock nullified and the ship shuddered with the last cough of the engine burn. The gentle hiss of the carbon scrubbers and slight hum of the dehumidifier arose in the new level of quiet.

That was it. The last of the maneuvering fuel was spent and he had achieved orbit. The computer softly whined about the empty fuel tanks and he silenced the alarm. There were other things to think about.

The red planet loomed outside the window, the giant red eye of a demon peering in at him.

"Hello," Helios said to the window.

He sighed as he began to transfer the fuel from the landing module tanks into the ship's drained maneuvering systems. He had waited until the very last minute before making the transfer and admitting finally that he wasn't going to land on the planet after all. "Sorry I can't stay," he added wistfully.

The mottled ochre surface rolled away from him. It felt like the red welcome carpet was being yanked away from his boots. It wasn't fair. He'd won the race.

For at least a week he would own the whole planet. He would be the only human gazing down from the godlike height of orbit. The first to achieve orbit around Mars. But orbit wasn't the objective.

The crisp curve of night sleeved over the planet and he saw one pimply distortion against the advancing sunset. Olympus Mons stabbed a stubborn nose high above the plateau around it, sinking last into the rising flood of nightfall.

It would inevitably be Xiang Chu who would scale the highest peak in the solar system and plant the red flag of the People's Republic of China, making good on his promise to claim the red planet for the Chinese. Helios would watch from above, trapped in his front-row seat as Xiang Chu leapfrogged him into the history books.

The console blinked with notification of an incoming message and he felt a scrape along the inside of his spine. Where he had once craved contact with home and family, he now wished he could just climb under the rock of failure and hide. The six minute pauses in conversation added an extra excruciating dimension, each feeling like a remonstration. He punched the accept button. Even here, further away from Earth than any living human, he had nowhere to hide.

"Helios, you're first to Mars. Congratulations." It was Finn, his flight director, formerly just his VP of Operations for the small collection of connected rocket casings on the moon that they called Lunae Clara and enticed vacationers from Earth to visit. "Just a warning, though: you're about to get some company. Xiang's ship is damaged."

Helios quickly stabbed the console. "Explain." He said simply, eager to send his message back to Earth as quickly as possible.

For twelve minutes he waited for the signal to crawl to Earth and the answer to crawl back. In the meantime his heart thudded as he grappled with the implications. How damaged could Xiang's ship be? Would he need a rescue? Would he be able to land on Mars? Could there be somewhere in the infinite muck of space a distant starlight of hope that Helios' own failure would be absolved by the travesty impeding Xiang?

"A micrometeorite nailed the coolant distribution system of his main landing retro thruster. The impact caused a pressure spike that actually burst the relief valve and drained all his coolant. He can't land. You can see how this changes the situation."

For twelve minutes there was only Helios, the impassive

face of the dead planet, and his heart thudding with hope.

This did change the situation. Helios had the only functional landing system in orbit around Mars, but not enough fuel to get home. Xiang would have fuel enough for a landing and return to Earth, but no way to land on Mars. Finn's voice crackled on the speakers just as Helios thought it to himself:

"There's a deal to be made."

*

Xiang Chu was coming. Somewhere in the vast cauldron of space surrounding Helios one of the bright specks was the Chinese ship, hurtling toward him. Helios waited, turning about the planet like a predator pacing his cage. With each minute his imagination reminded him that Xiang was closer, creating a palpable pressure on his temples as his heart rattled with adrenaline. The only other time in the voyage he had felt the neck-and-neck racer's anxiety was when he had overtaken Xiang and they had passed within six thousand kilometers of each other.

The Chinese trillionaire had ensured his victory from the moment he had announced his intention to travel to Mars by revealing himself only months before his launch. The world was stunned.

The only prospect for competition was Helios' ferries carrying tourists back and forth to the fledgling colony on the moon, the only extra-orbital craft in operation. His ships were space-worthy but lacked the fuel capacity and ability to travel to Mars, maneuver into orbit, land on the surface and take off again. It took unlimited resources from a suddenly cooperative and inspired US Space Agency and over a year to get a newly engineered mars lander module into orbit and attached to Helios' craft.

Helios' team, knowing they could never launch before Xiang, created a faster path to Mars. Six modules of fuel and oxygen were launched from Earth in escalating elliptical orbits designed to intersect with Helios' modified trajectory to Mars. Helios would rendezvous with each stepping stone, refilling his tanks and burning to steeper and faster transfer orbits than Xiang.

One such rendezvous is like long distance darts from the back of a moving truck. Six was ambitious. The problem occurred on the sixth rendezvous. Any of the possible failures in mathematics, mechanics of the craft, or collision with debris occurred. All Helios found at the time and place of rendezvous was the continuing yawning indifference of infinite space. Just like that he had no fuel for landing on Mars.

Now, in orbit around Mars, Helios would finally have his sixth rendezvous, only it wouldn't be with the familiar stepping stone cylinder crammed with fuel, oxygen and music. This time it would be with the growing speck of light that revealed itself to be Xiang Chu's ship, a spread eagled spider of solar wings with an ant's body of modules lined up at the hub.

The spider crept closer to Helios over the course of the final day, both ships racing around the red planet as their computers nudged them together. The slow approach gave Helios the opportunity to study the Chinese craft and its shattered landing craft. A hole had been gnashed out of the ship's flank, leaving trailing ends of twisted conduit and a shredded corner of a balloon cushion dangling in space.

The ships embraced at last with the gasketted kiss of docking collars. Clamps engaged and the airlock ready indicator gleamed green. Helios prepared to meet his rival, focusing himself on the possible bargain he could make for fuel.

*

"There's a little bit more room aboard my ship," Helios radioed casually to Xiang, "why don't you come aboard?" He unconsciously looked upward and tried to control his breathing as he waited for the Taikonaut's response. Helios hoped to control the bargaining from the first moment by having Xiang come to him. It was crucial that Helios make this work and get the fuel he needed to finish the mission. Xiang would no doubt be just as eager to engineer his own way through Helios and down to the planet. Far from Earth and on the stoop of greatness, the two men would have to negotiate victory on behalf of billions of hopeful people back home.

Xiang obligingly slid through the airlock. It was toward afternoon of Helios' ship time and Helios immediately wondered if a dinner invitation would strengthen the natural authority he was attempting to create as a host. On the other hand, he was aware that his food offerings were embarrassingly limited and the aura of poverty would ruin him. He pushed the thoughts away and focused on Xiang instead.

"Hello, Mr. Collins," Xiang said smoothly, somehow maintaining excellent posture and balance in the cramped ship while he extended his hand to Helios. Xiang had a slight frame, short and tightly-controlled black hair and he wore a spotless and almost magically crisp white jumpsuit. The wrinkles in Helios' own suit crumpled his authority somewhat. Helios braced himself and took Xiang's hand.

"Hi," Helios answered simply. "Welcome aboard the Lunar Transit, Mr. Chu. Perhaps sometime you'll be able to take a trip in her to my moon city."

Xiang's eyes glittered as he scanned the ship, his expression unchanging. "An interesting notion, Mr. Collins." Something in the fixed smile that never touched the Chinaman's eyes made Helios shiver. The man's eyes locked on Helios. "I'd much rather take her to Mars."

Right to it then. Helios had to admit he was a little taken aback.

"Well," Helios answered, "there are a few facts here: one,

only my ship can land, and two, only I can fly it."

Xiang's smile widened temporarily. "Rest assured, Mr. Collins, my people have been able to make me thoroughly familiar with your ship's systems in the last six months. It is not that...sophisticated."

Helios' glare ricocheted off the granite countenance of Xiang. Mars rolled away beneath them, a boiling red egg in a magma glow. The scrubbers hissed and a compressor hummed into life as it cooled the humidity out of the air. Helios took a deep breath and stretched a smile over his face.

"Look, it's been a long voyage, for both of us. This whole situation really is a God-given opportunity. You and I are in the unique position of being able to be the start of an incredible relationship between Chinese and American people. The cooperation we do today is going to be an example for generations to come."

It was the most magnificent thing Helios had ever said.

Xiang sniffed. "You have a ship without fuel that you won't let anyone else fly. For me to give you that fuel so that you can complete your task and make me fail mine is ludicrous."

"It's the only way. To have us both return home with neither landing on the surface would be a deep embarrassment to the human race. We would become icons of hubris."

"You worry about embarrassment. If you will not give me your ship then I am just worried about how rich I can get with the fuel that I have."

Helios sucked in a breath, suppressing a simultaneous cheer and shudder. He knew at that moment that he would be going to the planet. He would make history. Yet, knowing what he knew about business, he also knew it was going to cost him almost as much as the prize. He was too giddy to care.

"Name it," Helios said brazenly.

Xiang just grinned. The smile did touch his eyes now, a

frightening visceral glitter, and Helios suddenly thought of the victorious snap of a Venus fly trap. He realized that Xiang had known how this was going to play out before he had entered orbit. Helios had shown just how badly he wanted to land on the planet and now all he could do was wait for the teeth of the trap to chomp down on him.

"Very well, Mr. Collins, I'll take the moon."

Helios felt each hair from the very base of his spine to the tip of his neck stand consecutively at attention. Ice water flooded through his body, sluicing down from his chest through to his toes.

"What?" Was all Helios could manage.

Xiang nodded understandingly and then spoke again more slowly, locking his eyes on Helios to enforce his deadly earnestness.

"Lunae Clara, your city on the moon, your ships, your Earth space terminus – your entire space business – is to be mine."

It punched Helios all over again. He swallowed, but a thick raw lump clogged his throat and he tried to wheeze a breath through it.

"That's everything – "

"And," the single word slapped Helios, leaving him wordlessly working his mouth as his eyes widened in horror for the Chinaman's next words. He felt the agony of endurance when the peak of pain was revealed to only be a step in the crescendo. Xiang waited, building the potential energy of the next blow. "And, the flag you will plant at the peak of Olympus Mons will be the Chinese flag."

"No," Helios said reflexively. The image was already burning in his mind – the wide red Martian horizon broken only by the red flag of China snapping triumphantly in the ever-present Martian winds, dutifully carried there by American labour sent by the Chinese to do their work. America would be furious. Xiang would be the hero who not only planted China's flag on the surface but dominated Americans to do so

The Chinese would not consider the moon a second place prize, either. Helios well knew how the Chinese inherently adored the moon. They were some of his top-paying customers, especially eager to travel during the Autumn Moon Festival, and otherwise considered it life-changing good luck voyage.

Even as he said no, Helios instantly regretted it. That fear of losing the deal confirmed to him what Xiang had already known; that Helios needed to be on that planet, to make for himself a legacy so tall that the weight of his footsteps would be among those that turned the very Earth around its axis. Helios knew he could not abide flying so close to the surface, staring from orbit at the clear outlines of canyons and dust storms, so close he could imagine dangling his fingers out the window and drawing his fingers through the dust below, but not setting his boot down. He needed to feel that cereal crunch of his heel commanding his place onto a brand new world for Man.

Xiang raised his eyebrows. "No?" He asked, the slight draw upward of one side of his mouth mocking Helios.

Helios was trembling. He wiped his forehead. A detached portion of his mind marveled at the amount of sweat staining his blue jumpsuit sleeve black. He watched as Xiang calmly opened a pocket on the leg of his jumpsuit and pulled out a square of red cloth. Carefully, he extended the folded cloth to Helios. On the top fold was a large golden star. The Chinese flag.

Helios reached out his hand. His hand shook, his guts felt completely emulsified and he thought every bone in his body must have been steamrolled into a paper thin leaf by the collision of his burning desire and the weight of future generations of critical analysis of his decision. This is what making history feels like, he thought.

He took the flag in his left and held out his wobbling right hand. Xiang's cool hand compressed his knuckles and raised them in one curt, obliging handshake.

It was done. Helios was going to Mars.

*

Once in his suit, Helios scooted feet-first into the landing module and pulled the hatch shut behind him. Automatically, he confirmed that the fuel had been transferred back from his ship's maneuvering engines and into the lander's engines. Xiang's ship would in turn provide the fuel for the burn to escape orbit and fly back to Earth.

The release from the command module felt like an accidental snap as the lander lurched sideways and was suddenly adrift with that irreversible freedom of pushing away from a shore.

Rapid punches of pressurized hydrogen shot from the multi-axial jets banding the hull as the automated system flipped Helios on his back and steadied him for the plunge. He waited, unconsciously holding his breath as at the top of a roller coaster. The landing engine fired without warning, and he felt like a lion was stepping on his chest and roaring into his face.

Through the entire turbulent descent Helios fought back the feeling that maybe Xiang had tricked him. They had formalized the deal with a transmission back to Earth, so Helios was no longer the owner of Lunae Clara. Could Xiang have sabotaged the craft? Would he have? Would the humiliation of America be victory enough for him?

Density changes in the air he collided with banged on the hull and shook the whole ship, feeling like a bomb planted to kill him and break the ship to pieces. He ground his teeth together, trying to stow the feeling he was going to die, but the constant rattling and shaking only made his teeth batter each other.

The landing was far worse than he imagined, based on the simulation and descriptions. The retro rocket exploded in a short and desperate decimation of his acceleration, feeling like a kick in the back and forcing his skull back onto his headrest. The engine exhausted itself and then it was weirdly quiet as his stomach raised with the feeling of dropping all over again and the wind began to whistle around the hull again.

The second stage and impact seemed to happen all at once. Airbags snapped to life all around him and he lost every ounce of wind in his chest as the ship hit. Then he was tumbling, gasping, rolling and screaming in a jolting mess of deflating airbags and rolling spaceship that he could only describe as like being in a laundry dryer.

It all stopped, only the quiet sounds left: the ticking of the superheated metal contracting under the minus 60 Celsius atmosphere, the faint rush of wind over the hull and windows.

Unfortunately, Helios did not emerge from the spacecraft with any of the slow, breathless care of Neil Armstrong. After beating the ship's hatch open, Helios instead rolled out of the capsule like a half-dead slug, landing face-first on the floor of the new world and lying still while the curious Martian wind picked him over, flicking some red dust over his helmet and suit.

His first awareness of the planet wasn't the crunch of the soil under his boot as he had always imagined. It was the sound. After finally corralling his breath and sitting upright he struggled to interpret the faraway, tinny sound of the wind. Sounds were muted, he realized, by the thinness of the atmosphere. The wind scooped up clouds of dirt right in front of him and piled it onto his lap but sounded miles away.

He focused on his hand on the ground. He had pushed himself up with his glove palm-down on the surface and now he noticed the cold grainy squish of the dirt as he pulled his fist closed and lifted the dirt up to his helmet. It poured from his hand with an eerie slowness. He almost lapsed into a trance from the sudden peacefulness after the landing and the sublime contentment of finally accomplishing his mission.

"Hello, Mars," he said, "I made it." A sudden rush of panic gripped him as he realized he had just flushed away his chance to say some epic first words for all of humanity to cherish. As least he hadn't cursed.

The craft had helpfully landed on the gently sloping flank of the mountain Helios was to climb. Thankfully, the highest mountain in the solar system was a shield volcano, a flatter, wider type of volcano that presented few obstacles other than being roughly the size of Arizona and three times the height of Everest. Even using the rover that Helios unpacked from the landing craft, it took him over eight hours to reach the 60 kilometer-wide caldera gaping at the peak.

With only twenty hours of oxygen in his tanks, Helios did not have a lot of time to spend on the lip of the caldera. He allowed himself the chance to peer over the massive edge, feeling almost pulled into the enormous maw of the three kilometer deep crater.

His radio beeped. He mashed his glove against the receive button.

"Eagle Two, this is Heavenly Sun. We read your position at the summit. Are you prepared to transmit? Will relay to Earth."

Helios bounced over to the edge of the crater in line with the camera on the rover dashboard that had been recording every minute of his journey. A small button on his suit would activate the transmitter and send the camera signal to his ship for Xiang to relay to Earth. He struggled with the flag pole first, positioning the pole over bare bedrock before engaging the explosive-powered rock bolts that fired anchors directly into the rock. The red flag unfolded and flapped lazily in the thin air. Feeling a pang of irritation that it wasn't the American flag screaming pride across the solar system, he knelt down and scooped together several large stones, stacking them in an unmistakably deliberate pyramid. At least with that he felt a sense of contribution of his own. Helios pressed the button.

Despite losing his entire fortune and risking the enmity of the entire American population forever, Helios couldn't keep the jubilation from his tone as he addressed Earth. Standing there on the edge of the enormous mouth of the volcano, distant tendrils of windswept dust ghosting behind him while the red dirt stained his entire suit and his helmet gleamed chrome and alien red, he felt the supreme joy of standing higher and further than anyone in Time had before. He knew then that he would never regret it. He would never want that moment undone, where he had stood beside that flag and the small stack of stones that proved that Men had been there. He knew then that what people on Earth thought of him didn't matter. He was more Martian now than any of them anyway.

Red Sleepers
By T. Fox Dunham

"Come right in, Molasses Love!" Aunt Sadie said. "Make yourself at home." Sadie always said that to Liz when she came to her antebellum mansion in the Okefenokee swamps of Georgia. Oak moss draped the cypress trees and oaks, falling like antiquated wedding veils over branches, hiding the faces of the trees. Liz always wanted to be married one day, but she didn't know which one of them would wear the veil, her or her wife. Perhaps they both could wear woven crowns of oak moss and sassafras leaves, decorating her golden hair. She had to shave it before the mission, and the grumpy machines fed growth suppressants into her body to keep her from aging in stasis, keeping her head shorn.

"Aunt Sadie?" The crone waved from the front porch of the house, holding herself up on the cracked white pillars. Not many of these large houses survived past the year 2025. Most private houses had been demolished for unit living—clean, small and affordable to the massive population that spread over the planet like a virus.

"Come on in and tell me all about your adventures." Liz wore a white dress, simple like she liked them and walked bare feet in the grass as she did when she was a little girl, visiting her aunt, escaping the smog and pollution of the industrial north. Her asthma had been acting up, and her parents sent her south for some fresh air. She ran for the house, eager for biscuits and fresh milk. Then, Liz remembered.

"I can't, Aunt Sadie."

"Why ever not? Come on in and tell me all about your life. I just want to hear your stories and your stories of your kin."

"Because you died, Aunt Sadie. I'm so sorry. But you drowned in this house. Georgia is under the sea after Hurricane

47

Marjorie. The earth is drowning."

"Oh. I see then. Saints!"

The alarm sounded in Liz's head. The dream evaporated. The comforts of the warm seasons declined, and she shivered. Her throat seized. Jelly spilled into her lungs, and her body jerked, throwing her against the container lid. The seal departed—part of the reanimation sequence—and Liz pushed herself out of the chemical solution. The gelatin oozed down her limbs. She shook with chills.

"Commander Sun," Plato said through a synthesized voice. "Good morning."

She coughed out the gelatin. Her throat throbbed. Liz found a robe in a plastic bag hanging from the tank and covered her naked body. She'd lost weight on the trip. The International Science Council promised that wouldn't happen, but she could see the loss in her stomach and wondered if she had time to find a mirror. Liz reached for her hair and found it missing. "Status?" she rasped.

"Earth date: June 21st 2052. Minor power fluctuations in the fusion plant due to magnetic disturbances from solar flares. Communications beacon transmitting. Engines—"

"Stow it," she ordered. "Are we here?"

"Positive value. Exodus 3 made planet-fall on Mars three months and three days ago."

She stretched her limbs, still groggy and stiff, reminding Liz of waking on the train in Georgia as a girl, having slept half the trip. "Life support?"

"Crew and colonists all stable and in stasis."

"We all survived?" Three hundred humans slept in similar tanks in the hold, dreaming of a better world, a future. This was a one way trip for them, and they'd consume the basic materials of their ship to build the first colony on the red planet—but not for another century. They'd sleep through some basic terra-forming to conserve supplies, let the automated systems drill for ice and produce enough liquid water for oxygen and fuel. Earth would probably hold on. "Check the life values of Connor Sun."

"Connor Sun is stable." She sighed. Liz had vowed to protect her little brother since Marjorie drowned their mother and father. She'd given up her youth to take care of him. That's what family did. "Maybe there's a god watching us somewhere in the darkness of the universe." She'd pulled every string to assign her brother to the exodus. He had no particular skills except for his art, his beautiful sculptures. It brought tears to her eyes when she envisioned the rusty red statues he'd shape and mold from the Martian soil. They couldn't just survive here and function if they were to live as a people. The new race had to possess soul, art, music, literature; or what was the point? Scientists, doctors, and engineers filled the cargo hold, but the artists were their true treasure and had to be protected at all costs.

"I am not programmed for theology," Plato announced. She swore the artificial intelligence pouted. "But there are several leaders of various earth religions who can be of better service to you in stasis. Would you like me to wake one of them?"

"Disregard," she said. Liz dried herself off with a disposable towel then tossed it into the recycle chute. "Display status hologram." A photodiode ignited on the display panel and projected a sphere from the central console on the bridge. Automated systems controlled the ship and really didn't require a human operator, but perhaps because of vanity or ego, she had been placed in command—Noah guiding her cargo through the deluge. The council put them to sleep on earth's moon before the launch, and she'd woken up here. Liz ran her fingers over the holographic sphere. The sensation of the sections tingled with various vibrations, reporting their current status. She ran a diagnostic on the power plant then checked the levels of helium 3 and deuterium. The variances in the core forced the plant to consume more fuel to compensate, but they still had enough resources to run the plant for another fifty years—enough time to mine the hydrogen they needed and receive new shipments from earth. Two cargo vessels should already be *en route*.

"Open communications," she said.

Plato hesitated. "Communication's beacon is transmitting but not receiving."

"Run a diagnostic." She checked the transmitter again on the display.

"All systems operational."

"What about radio signals? Anything on the EM band?"

"Negative," Plato said. "Solar flare activity is creating significant interference."

"When did the activity begin?" she asked Plato.

"A few hours after we made planet-fall," Plato reported. "Magnetic fields have caused sensors to malfunction."

"The ship's magnetic shield emitter is functioning?" Exodus 3 was designed with an EM generator that would protect the crew and cargo from solar flares and cosmic radiation.

"Emitter operating at 80% efficiency," Plato stated.

"That's a tad low," Liz said.

"I am currently running a diagnostic. There is an imbalance in the coil of the emitter. An external repair might be required. I will dispatch a disposable automated unit if it falls below 70%."

"We only have so many of those, and I'd get quite toasty outside the ship's field in a solar flare."

The commander picked some gel from her skin and scanned the cramped cabin, orientating herself to the ship. Liz had viewed the schematics many times in preparation for the mission, but the ship hadn't been completed when they went into stasis. The parts were manufactured in space and shot at the moon where they were assembled. The job had to be rushed before society's infrastructure collapsed.

Liz would deal with this later. She had a job to do, a planet to create. She checked the terra-forming pods. As soon as they landed, the vessel launched automated vehicles, robotic creatures who would move out onto the Martian surface and dig, burning chemical components in the soil, heating up the planet exactly as humans had done to ruin the Earth—this time to bring the planet to the right conditions for life, not destroy it. "Time for sleep. Sing me a lullaby?"

"I am not coded for that service," Plato said. "But there are several musicians in stasis. I could reanimate one of them—"

"That's okay," she said, taking off her robe and shivering. "Aunt Sadie will sing me to sleep." The commander reset the automated systems, deactivated the displays. The cabin darkened. "You'd think they would have installed a window."

"Cabin pressure concerns—"

"Goodnight, Connor. See you soon." She sighed, dipped a foot into the vat of gel and dove in, lying flat in what she tried not to think of as a glass coffin. Aunt Sadie used to tell her the story of Snow White. Perhaps some princess would come along and kiss her back to life. *Don't hold your breath.* Liz inhaled the gelatin. Her lungs ached, and she resisted the urge to choke. The gel also served as an electrode, monitoring her biological functions, feeding her low levels of nutrients and oxygen. The chemicals induced her stasis, and she slept.

*

"How's your pie coming along, Molasses Darling?" Aunt Sadie asked. Liz smelled sweet strawberries baking in her Aunt's old fashioned gas oven. She sat in her Aunt's kitchen, sipping tea at her table. Aunt Sadie wore a flowery spring dress that barely covered her wide hips. She'd never had children and had gone through a series of husbands before finally calling it quits. She didn't need a man to be complete but enjoyed their company like having a pet. Liz always admired her strength.

"I've not tasted strawberries since I was a girl."

"The county folk are going to say I'm biased because my niece is in the contest, so I've got to judge your pie fairly. I hope you understand that."

"Of course, Aunt Sadie." But she winked at Liz.

"It's for a major prize. All the money. Everything. The whole enchilada."

"I'll make you proud," Liz said.

"Just prove yourselves worthy," Sadie said and sipped from her tea. The gray shade of her eyes changed, turning violet, growing somehow, scanning through Liz. The alien sensation disturbed Liz, but her aunt's eyes morphed back to normal. Liz shook it off.

"It's really good to see you again," Liz said, taking her aunt's spotty hand.

"And you, Molasses, but you surprise me. I've always been here. Forever and ever, since the world was born."

"My world?" Liz asked.

"My world," Aunt Sadie said. "And maybe yours . . ."

Liz sipped her tea, tasting the bitterness and sweet, the tannins and leaves. She'd never dreamed in such vivid detail before. Dreams always feel like your own mind, your own thoughts directing and creating, but this world felt independent of her and not the creation of her fears, her desires, all the mental detritus that produces nightly reveries.

"Am I still on the Exodus?" she asked.

"You better check your pie, dear," Sadie said. "You don't want it to burn." Liz got up and opened the oven. The pie crust was evenly tanned. It would only need to bake for a few more minutes. She wanted to relax but couldn't shake the feeling that something was off.

"This is more than a dream," Liz said.

"Your body is still on your moving rock," Sadie said. "But

your mind joined with the fields and flows, the ebbs and tides that flow from my heart." Aunt Sadie put on a sweater. "Now come on. We're going to be late for the contest." Liz blinked, and the room vanished. She stood at a table covered in various pies and baked goods. Numbers marked each one. Faceless folk moved to and fro, but she didn't recognize any of them, never got a good look into their eyes. Judges at the head table all looked away, all but her Aunt Sadie. The skies darkened, threatening rain. A deluge approached. Aunt Sadie stood up. Her eyes morphed again. A crimson landscape flowed through her irises. Rusty dust blew in her vision. "I'd like to ask my niece a few questions," Sadie said.

"What are you really?" Liz asked. "Are you an alien? Am I going crazy?"

"I am this body," Aunt Sadie said, her voice changing. "I have been asleep. Once I flowed with water and green lush with life, but my breathing changed. I couldn't hold my air. I watched my sister world grow with children and loved her from afar."

"You're our Aunt Mars?"

Aunt Sadie smiled, showing her false teeth.

"I've been watching all this time," the old lady said. "I've watched life come and go on your world. Your race showed so much promise. You've made quite the home on my sister. But why have you come here?"

Liz realized she entreated with a powerful being, some kind of archetype goddess: maternal spirit of this planet. She didn't know how powerful her Aunt was or what kind of influence she held over the ship or the sleepers, but Liz understood she had to step carefully. This contest was symbolic, a metaphor of what really transpired. They were being judged as a species, and Liz had to do everything she could to ensure their survival, even lie; yet, could she deceive? This ancient spirit lived in Liz's head.

53

She would know, and would they really be worthy of survival if she had to lie? Liz had to do this the honorable way, be the best of what her race could be.

"Our world is changing," she said. "The water is rising. Storms are flooding the continents. The air is changing. We are suffocating."

"Did you cause this to my sister and your world?" Aunt Sadie asked.

Liz's response shamed her. "We did over time. We polluted the air and changed the ecosystem. And . . . we knew what we were doing but wanted to be comfortable. We have suffered for it. Our home is drowning. We've come here to start again. I've lost contact with my race. We might be the last."

"You can be a shortsighted people," Aunt Sadie said. She frowned and lowered her head. "I am asleep and only need to be awakened. I can be lush and alive, safe and beautiful. I can give you a second chance. But I must consider if I will allow you to stay and not give another species a chance."

The dream ended, and Liz awoke in her vat. Alarms buzzed in her head, and she vomited the gelatin. The lid opened, and she pulled herself out of the box. Holographic interfaces flashed red. Wave patterns glowed from the emitters, illuminating the walls of the cabin.

"Plato. Status!"

"Magnetic field and radiation increasing. Sensors are malfunctioning. Probable cause: Solar flare activity. Shield has fallen below 70%."

"It's not solar flares," Liz said, working the hologram, trying to accumulate data through the malfunctioning eyes of the ship.

"Radiation rising to lethal levels. The crew will not survive."

"It's coming from the planet. This is intentional." Liz worked the consoles, playing the holographic interface like a piano. She worked fast, trying to keep the shield steady. It dropped to half strength. Liz reached for her hair and growled when she couldn't find it. The shield shouldn't have been falling so fast, and she suspected interference. Humans had been judged unworthy, but she wasn't going to lie down and just sleep like some lost princess. "Release the automated repair unit."

"Remote interface not functional. The EM fields are interrupting internal systems. Working."

She banged the control panel with her fist. "How long before the radiation kills our cargo?"

"Lethal damage to biological systems will occur within ten to twelve minutes."

Visions of her brother asleep in bed crossed her mind when they lived in that tiny unit in PhilaYork. The cities dug their tentacles into the earth, massing over the continents. She'd gone to wake him during the evacuation when the sea walls collapsed, and she couldn't find their breathing filters. She'd promised Connor he'd survive.

Liz unsealed the hatch to the access tube. An environmental suit hung the wall—an empty body needing a soul. She planned to imbue it with spirit. "I'll be the first human to walk on the surface of Mars," she said. "The first woman."

"Commander. You will have to correct the variance in the emitter coils. This will require you to work outside the hull and the protection of the ship's EM shield."

She first put on a jumpsuit then fit the heavy gloves and boots on her extremities. "We won't have a field if I don't." The rest of the suit fit like pieces of armor, locking into place. Liz inserted the helmet onto the neck plate. It pressurized. A head's up display glowed in her visor. A tool box emerged from the wall. She picked it up, and the box felt light. Servos in the suit limbs enhanced strength and coordination. Liz manually operated the airlock. She stepped into the venue, and the hatch sealed behind her. The pristine white of the walls glowed like a sterile hospital room, and she released the latch to the bulkhead then took her first steps onto crimson sands.

Come and rest a spell! She remembered her Aunt Sadie used to say.

"We are worthy," she said. The sand crunched under her boot like compacted snow. Her visor tinted, shielded her eyes, and Liz gazed out onto the red desert. Water erosion from melting ice producing aquifers under the rocky surface smoothed out cheeks and jowls and mouths from the inchoate landscape. Olympus Mons rose its giant head in the distance— the perfect location to drill out dwelling space below the protective mountain.

"You should make your way up the tertiary access," Plato said through her helmet transceiver. "Radiation levels increasing. You are now outside the ship's EM shield."

"Aunt Sadie always had a temper," Liz said.

"Commander?"

"Right," she said. Liz attached the case to her suit and climbed up spokes along the side of the vessel, pulling her bulky suit up the side of the rectangular compartment. The units of the ship reminded her of an apartment building built at odd angles, jutting out from different sides of a central skeleton. Pods hung along the sides of the infrastructure, built into the polymer lattice. She hurried, racing the digital radiation gauge filling like a cistern on her HUD. It registered half the lethal range. Liz had minutes. "It's not fair," she said. "Everyone deserves a second chance."

"I am not coded for philosophical debates," Plato said. "But if you like, I can reanimate a member of—"

"You're doing that on purpose now," she said, reaching the array. She pulled out a diagnostic device from the box and plugged it into the port on one of the three discs that had been built into the transmitter.

"EM shield down to 30%," Plato reported. "Life support failing."

Liz's fingers numbed as she worked the diagnostic—the first effects of the EM radiation. Her thoughts clouded, and her thoughts blurred. Liz missed the controls a few times and had to focus to finish the process. She fetched an EM Stabilizer from the kit. It should be the right tool to balance the inductance built in the system and allow for free flow. A shadow darkened the hull, and she looked up at a floating rock: Phobos. Seeing the Martian sky was worth just a few minutes of life.

"Molasses," her Auntie Sadie spoke in Liz's head. "Why don't you come in from the storm and get yourself warm. I'll make you a nice cup of tea."

"I'd love to, Auntie," Liz said. "But I've got a job to do first." Her heart accelerated, banging in her ears. Her suit warned her that her health functions failed. The EM field cooked her neurons and fried her nerves. She felt like she was falling.

"But why give up your life? It's all a bunch of silliness."

"Because I promised," Liz said. The numbness spread up her arms and neck. Her thoughts scattered. Liz finished running the bar over the discs.

"Ship EM field efficiency increasing. 40%. 50%. Rising."

Liz collapsed in the suit and shut her eyes.

"Wake up now, Molasses," Aunt Sadie said. "I think that'll be sufficient."

Liz awoke in the gelatin. The lid peeled back from the stasis pod. The commander yanked herself out of the solution, shivering and spit up the goo. "Plato. Status of EM shield."

"Operating at peak efficiency," he stated.

"I corrected the malfunction? How did I end up back in stasis?" She wondered if one of the automated systems had come online and fetched her from the hull.

57

"What malfunction?" Plato asked.

"I left the ship to fix the array," she said, finding her robe.

"I have no record of any crew departure from the ship," Plato informed her. "Perhaps you were dreaming."

"It wasn't real," she said, confirming her theory through the holographic display. "Aunt Sadie was testing me. I never woke up." Was it enough? Liz sensed this wasn't the only test of the human species but the first of many. She would tell her people about the spirit of the world that had slept like they were sleeping, how she'd be watching. They had their second chance, starting from the cradle again, walking on a new world with new hope.

So Liz returned to her pod and slept, to be awoken at intervals to check the systems. Would she hear from Earth again? Or should she let go of the past?

She dreamed of violet skies and red grass.

Observations From The Black Ball Line Between Deimos And Callisto

By Alexandra Erin

There are no seasons in space,
they say, but they've never been.
Earth-bound poets project their own lack
of imagination onto the black,
say it has no romance, no rhythm.

The food is good,
the old joke says,
but it's got no atmosphere.

They were telling that one on Earth
before the first foot fell on the first moon,
and they're still telling it to this day.
Only the venue has changed.

They're wrong on every count, including the food.
The food is usually indifferent, often terrible,
nothing special at its decadent best.
It's not always freeze-dried,
not always vacuum-locked,
not always so loaded with stabilizers
it has more aftertaste than taste,
but it's never fresh, neither.

You don't go to space for the food.

You go for the atmosphere.

You go for viewpoints you never find on earth,
for the chance to say you were there,
for the freedom of weightlessness,
the awesome power of acceleration
when you make your first burn
at the start of a push.

Out in the black,
gravity comes in extremes,
very little or all at once.
I'd say you get used to it,
but it hasn't happened yet.

There are no seasons in space
they say, but they've never been.
They've never been there on
Deimos Station six months before
Mars reaches Jovian perigee.
That's when the push begins,
when shipping containers fitted
with retro rockets are launched
like cannonballs across the void.

Unmanned crates outnumber manned,
by more and more every year.
Drones burn hotter, push harder,
take g-forces no human body could.

Some things always take
the human touch, though.

Humans, for instance.

Live passengers.

Sweet sentimentality,
precious cargo of
precious keepsakes.

It keeps us in business,
the need to have a human
riding shotgun on a cannonball
fired and forgotten in the void,
the need to know someone
is standing by the helm,
ready to spring into action
when things go elliptical.

Space travel is sharpshooting.
It calls for marksmen, not ace pilots.
We take aim for the future,
not for where our target is,
but where it will be when we get there.
They're all moving targets out here,
but their motions were plotted
when our ancestors sailed the seas.

No need for keen eyes or quick reflexes
when your target is as big as a moon
and steady as a calendar.

No room for hotshots when every maneuver
means burning up your delta-v.

There's always a margin of error
on the black ball line,

but the wider you make it,
the thinner the profit.
No one lives this life for the money,
but you still need money to live it.

There may be no romance
in the cold calculations
of lift and thrust,
but there is danger,
and that's similar.

The poets back on earth
got it all wrong from the beginning.
They've never stopped resenting us
for not dancing between the stars,
for not sailing the void
on a wave of light and fire
with a whoosh and a zoom
and a lens flare twinkling impishly
at an improbable observer.
After centuries of space travel,
they still expect noisy laser battles
that weave in and out of asteroid fields.

We're no more or less between the stars than you are back
on Earth.
The nearest one is that much farther away from us than it is
from you.

Lasers are for sending, measuring,
finding our place in the trackless void.

You can't see them.
You can't hear them.
They can hurt as much
as a careless word,
but no more than that.

We mine asteroids, some of us,
but we never dodge them.
Sometimes a greenhorn
on their first cannonball run
asks what to do if they run into one,
but in all the years of slinging freight
between Deimos and Callisto
it's never come up once.

We still count years.
The diner on Deimos Station
is open twenty-four hours a day,
which just means "all the time"
and children wonder why we don't say so.

We have our seasons in the black
like you have seasons in the sun:

The slow season,
the busy season.
The freeze, the thaw.

After the perigee comes the harvest.
Months' of ships slung across the void
brake to a halt within days of each other.

At Phobos and Deimos,
at Callisto and Io and Ganymede,
at a dozen orbital overflow stations,
we all work, pilots and crews
alongside dock workers and stevedores.
Even Martian groundies get in on the act,
shifting freight to clear the bays
and bring the next load in
so the black ball crews
can turn their crates around
and make the trip back.

We mark shift's end
to keep our spirits up.
We celebrate each harvest
because we've earned it.

Then we climb into our crates
and we haul our asses home.
We haul other things, too.
It would be a crime not to.
Space is the one thing we have
too much of at both ends of the line.
You couldn't afford to make the run
if you showed up with a crate full of it.

The main thing is just to get yourself back.
No one wants to be stuck on the wrong end
when the freeze hits and the lanes shut down.
Midwinter's much the same on either end,
but there's no place like home for the holidays.
The poets on Earth got that much right.

When Jupiter's on the wrong side
of the sun from Mars,
it's winter on the black ball line.
The stream of ships making the run
thins and stretches out to nothing,
stragglers coasting on inertia
till it's time for their second burn,
the one that bleeds their
momentum off into the void
until they glide to a stop.
The final harvest comes
just before the freeze.

During the winter
little comes in,
nothing goes out.
We settle in.
We tell stories.
We sing songs.
We hoard rations,
make supplies last
until the blowout
in the middle of it all.
Solstice on the line.
Halfway out of the dark.

When the spring comes,
six months before Jovian perigee,
we take aim at the future once again.
We sling the ships carrying people,
material, Martian produce, Terran media,
out towards Jupiter and beyond..

Poets on earth always get it wrong
but we don't hold it against them.

How could they know?

They've never been.

We have poets of our own out here.
We have nothing but space
between Deimos and Callisto,
and we have nothing but words to fill it.

I'm a Little Teapot...
By Robert P. Hansen

"Approaching the coordinates, Sir," Ensign Ginger Busch said without looking up from the navigation console. "It's a small M-type asteroid. A very small one."

"How small?" Lieutenant Russell Conrad asked.

"About this big," she said, holding her hands about ten inches apart and squaring it.

"Terrific," he muttered. "Hardly worth the effort."

"Sir? The Commission was formed to clean up all the space junk between Mars and Earth, no matter how small it is."

"Yes, yes, I know," he replied. "I was hoping for something more significant." He sighed and added, "Match vectors and orient for grapple."

"Synchronicity will be achieved in approximately two minutes," she said. "We are still about five thousand kilometers from rendezvous."

"Let's see what it looks like," he said.

Ensign Busch activated the viewscreen and magnified it until the little asteroid was slowly rotating in its center.

"Funny," Lieutenant Conrad said. "From this angle, it looks a bit like a teapot."

Ensign Busch's eyebrows dipped down to the bridge of her nose as she squinted at the screen. "It does, doesn't it," she agreed.

"Have you heard of the celestial teapot?" Lieutenant Conrad asked.

"No," she replied. "Is it a constellation?"

Lieutenant Conrad smiled and shook his head. "No," he said, fighting off a chuckle. "It's an argument one of my namesakes proposed over a century ago."

"Your namesake?"

"Yes," he said, nodding. "Bertrand Russell. My father was a philosopher, and he revered Russell's analytic philosophy."

"Really?" she said. "What sort of argument was it?"

"It was an analogy," he said. "In his day, the dogmatic branch of religion claimed they could maintain their beliefs simply because they could not be proven wrong. In response to this, Russell showed that it was like believing in a teapot orbiting the sun simply because they lacked the telescopic technology to prove there wasn't one there. Of course, the Fundamentalists drew upon scripture to justify their claims, so he had to add the caveat that the source of his belief was scriptural in order to make it work."

"But the burden of proof falls on the one making the positive assertion," Ensign Busch objected. "It isn't possible to prove a universal negative."

"Exactly his point," he said. "Since they couldn't prove their claims, and since they wanted to maintain their beliefs despite the inability to prove them, they resorted to the tactic of claiming others had to prove them wrong. Of course, they believed *their* scripture was the literal truth as revealed by God, and to them that was legitimate evidence to justify their beliefs. Naturally, other religions had scripture too, but they dismissed *that* scripture as false."

"That isn't logically consistent," Ensign Busch said.

"That's what Russell said, too."

"Synchronized," Ensign Busch said. "Preparing to snag it."

Lieutenant Conrad watched the three-fingered grapple stretch out and slowly collapse about the asteroid. When the fingers touched it, the asteroid's rotation slowed and part of it flaked off.

"Easy now," he said. "I would prefer not to use the suction tube."

Ensign Busch frowned. "I don't think it was me," she said.

"It's the asteroid. It's a rubble pile. Sort of. Not really."

Lieutenant Conrad looked at her and frowned. "Would you mind explaining that?" he asked.

"Well," she said. "There's a hollow metal core, but the outer crust is an amalgam of loose stones and dust."

"It must have taken millennia to settle in such minimal gravity," Lieutenant Conrad said.

Ensign Busch nodded. "I'm surprised it captured anything at all."

"Can you magnify it a bit more?" he asked.

"Sure," she said, increasing the magnification tenfold. "What is it?"

"Can you shake off the rubble?"

She frowned for a moment, and then her fingers jumped from one button to another for several seconds. When she finished, the ship vibrated as a series of thrusters fired in quick succession. The grapple arm vibrated with the ship, and a small cloud of debris puffed out around the asteroid.

"Now, turn the ship a quarter turn to clear the asteroid from the dust cloud."

She did as instructed, and he shook his head. "I don't believe it," he said.

She looked up and stared at the viewscreen. "It's a teapot," she said. "One of those dainty ones they have in Japan for the tea ceremony."

"Yes," he said, moving a bit closer to the viewscreen. "What's that?" he asked, pointing at the base of the teapot.

"It looks like a logo," she said. "No," she corrected herself. "Not a logo. It's a word. 'Mad'?"

"No," Lieutenant Conrad said. "Made. They used to stamp the manufacturing location on the bottom of items. It probably is 'Made in China' or something like that. The grapple's finger is blocking the rest of it from our view."

"Want me to release it so we can find out?"

He nodded and watched the finger peel away. On the bottom of the teapot were stamped three simple words: **MADE BY GOD**.

After a few seconds, Lieutenant Conrad said, his voice hesitant and low, "Maybe I should change my name...."

Greenie
By David Castlewitz

Boy or girl, child or adult: Holder Sacket didn't care. The monster had to be killed. If Greenies were hulking, scaly fiends instead of hairless, round-faced bipeds, people like the inspector sent from Settlement Prime would despise them. But their short stature and humanoid form camouflaged their evil intent.

"Once we find it," Inspector Dora Gibbons said, "I'll be gone and you won't have to deal with me any longer."

Sacket turned his broad back to her, his hands on the porch railing and his soft blue eyes watching two drones hover above the spinning blades of a turbine. On the ground, a handful of rickety spiders lurched between rows of windmills.

"Ever been on a Greenie hunt?" Sacket said without looking back at the woman. He had a mental picture of her pinched face and close-set dark eyes. That was enough. He didn't need a fresh reminder of this interloper.

A three-wheeler pulled up and Sacket's eldest, Clement, jumped off the wide saddle. He darted up the wooden steps, his long legs easily taking them two at a time. "Got the fencing up, Miss Gibbons," he reported.

Sacket scowled, angry that the investigator had issued orders regarding the hunt. This was his farm. He and Clement and Clement's six siblings, even the three young girls, should be scouring the fields with shotguns and pitchforks, not setting up fences or watching video from the robot spiders.

"Good," Dora said. "We'll get some great intel if the thing starts running."

"That fence ain't tall enough," Sacket said. "That Greenie'll climb right over."

She gave him a small smile, her cheeks dimpling. "And right back into the forest. Which is what we'd all prefer, I'm sure."

Sacket shook his head. Once a Greenie became curious enough to invade a farm, the only way to keep it out was to destroy it. As a teenager newly off the transport ship, Sacket had enjoyed dozens of hunts that terrorized these aboriginals out of the grasslands and into the forests and the distant mountains.

"Anything else I should do?" Clement asked, and brushed his sun-drenched blonde hair away from his eyes. "Pop?" he added, turning to Sacket. And then, "Miss Gibbons?"

"I told you, it's Dora."

Sacket winced from the sight of the fingertip touch on the arm the woman gave his son. Clement's thick neck reddened. He scraped the toe of one boot against a post supporting the porch roof. A tall young man, he often drew a gush of pride from Sacket, who marveled at the family he and his now dead wife, Jean, created. Their three daughters were nearly as tall and strong-built as their four brothers. Together, they'd made their farm into a powerhouse with acres of turbines producing more than two terawatts of electricity for Settlement Prime as well as many of the ranches and agricultural centers surrounding it.

Which was why, Sacket reasoned, Prime shouldn't have sent this Dora Gibbons to interfere with what he knew should be done. How did they find out about the Greenie, anyway? None of his kids would've reported it. They knew better. Perhaps one of the day-workers?

"Want to spin with me?" Clement nodded towards his three-wheeler. "Take a run on the perimeter? You can do some spot readings." He pointed at the slate in Gibbon's hand.

"She can do her readings right here," Sacket said.

"But a spin on that Wheelie looks like fun," Dora countered. "Let's go." Again, the smile and the dimples. She gripped Clement's bare upper arm and he tapped her hand, then led her to the parked wheelie, where they climbed onto the saddle behind the large front wheel. She threw back her head, shook her shoulder-length brown hair, and put on the goggles Clement handed her, and then put her arms around the boy's waist.

The last thing Sacket wanted was for his eldest to get mixed up with someone from Prime. His sons and daughters were farm folk. Farm folk like their dead mother. He'd left the congested Martian Consortium with its concrete walls and tight quarters and gangs of men and women living on the government's dole so he could get away from Settlement types.

On the farm, he worked every day. In the Settlement, people like this Dora Gibbons worked a few days a year and spent the rest of their time doing nothing.

Sacket didn't want his kids mixed up with that kind. And neither would Jean, if she were alive. If she hadn't been killed by a Greenie.

*

"We've made a lot of progress in three days," Dora said, flashing her smile.

"And you've had two days more of my hospitality than you should," Sacket grumbled. He glanced at his three daughters, made a quick judgment about their attire. Modest enough flower-print tops, fitting for company. Each sat with downcast eyes, their attention on their evening fare. A mug-cat's howl pierced the silence. Long and high-pitched, the predator's call reached the house from the distant forest.

Clement said, "Come on, Pops. Dora's just doing what needs doing."

"Whatcha gonna do with the critter when you catch him," Sacket asked, punctuating his words with a jab of his fork.

"Take him back to the forest," Dora replied. "Tranquilize him, of course. Take his vitals and such, but then repatriate – "

"How do you know it's a him? Maybe we got a female and she's ready to drop a litter of pups."

73

"If you knew anything about Greenie culture and – "

"I know all I need to." Sacket sucked in a breath and glared at Clement to keep him quiet, to quell any thought of coming to this woman's defense. His three daughters, one by one, began to weep. They always did when he grew angry.

Dora spoke up. "We'll have your 'critter' – as you call him – in another day or so. He's isolated to sector seven and your boys and I moved the fence. He's surrounded." She drew a thin, palm-sized communicator from the side pocket of her bloused slacks.

Clement turned to Dora, an expectant and excited look on his broad face. His siblings sat poised on the edges of their seats, curiosity peppering their young faces.

Dora showed them the fuzzy picture on her communicator's screen. "Something moved."

"And you don't know what," Sacket said. "That's a flimsy fence." He pictured the tall stanchions clamped into their retainers. A good kick would disconnect the leg from its base. He'd watched on a monitor while his kids ran helter-skelter shoving supports point-first into the gritty soil, attaching the tall thin braces, and drawing the wire mesh tight.

"He won't escape," Dora said. "Then I'll be back to Prime and you can be on about your business."

And out of Clement's life. Sacket looked at his son's wide face, the soft blue eyes and softer blonde hair and the smooth curves of his cheekbones. His boy was too beautiful to waste on this narrow-faced shrew from Prime. His boy deserved the best, not some mediocre government functionary. His boy deserved a strong and able woman like his mother had been, a woman ready to help with the wind farm whether by negotiating a price for megawatts of power or supervising the building of a new wind turbine or clearing another acre of forest to increase output.

"I understand your viewpoint," Dora said.

"Do you?" Sacket snapped, an edge to his voice and a sneer on his lean face. He'd not shaved since she arrived. Nor had he showered. He wore a stained and rumpled brown jumpsuit from morning 'til night. On purpose. To rile her. Offend her. Let her know he didn't care a whit about her.

"Tell me," Sacket said, "Where you lived before you transported here, did you have rats running wild?"

Dora shook her head. A bit of color drained from her cheeks.

Sacket grinned. "What kind of vermin did you have, Inspector? And whatcha do? Coddle them? Understand them? Try to communicate with them?"

Dora set down her fork. "Greenies are intelligent aboriginals. The *original* inhabitants of this world, Mr. Sacket. Not the vermin you think they are."

One of the boys at the table spoke up. "Gray Roosies got cleared out of Zeta Two. Killed off. And they were smart. Intelligent, like you say."

Sacket grinned. Count on Jason, his youngest, to stick in his two bits. But it was Clement whom he wanted to hear speak. Clement should take his side.

Dora cleared her throat. "There are a lot of stories like that. A planet here and a planet there, all of them populated with original species that we don't take the time to understand." She pushed her bowl away, set her fork on the placemat woven from native plants, and stood.

"I can run you back to your cottage," Clement said. He'd done so the past two nights.

"It's a short walk," Dora said. "You don't have any giant gray-rats on the prowl, do you?"

"Just a Greenie," Sacket said.

"Thank you for the hospitality. For the meals these past few nights. For the cottage you've so generously provided." No twinkle in her eyes. No laugh or dimples now.

Sacket waved a hand at her, as though to say, No Problem, you're dismissed.

Dora walked out of the dining room, her footfalls loud on the polished floorboards. The door hinges creaked; the door shut with a click behind her.

Clement stood. "It's night, Pop. That's a ten minute walk. Maybe she don't know what Greenies can do, or she don't care, but we know. I know." He bolted from the table and grabbed a club from its hook on the wall, a battery-powered lantern, and a whistle to call for help.

"The rest of you, finish up, wash up, and get to bed," Sacket said to his brood once his eldest had gone. He glared at his unfinished bowl of stew. Gibbons had spoiled his appetite. The first night she'd eaten with them, she'd been quiet, listening and nodding, not commenting; that was the kind of guest he preferred. He liked visitors who knew their place and never contradicted anything he said.

Sacket stood and crossed to the small room off the larger one and looked in the weapons cabinet, which offered him the choice of an old-fashioned 12 gauge shotgun and a long-barreled small caliber revolver. Not the firepower he'd like, but Prime's arms control regulations limited what kind of weapons he could stock.

He took his favorite, the revolver, and, strapped on a holster and shoved a box of cartridges in his overalls pocket. He added a club and a lantern to light the way, and then left the house. His children traded conjectures and childish complaints the moment he opened the front door. He let the clamor spill behind him.

*

Forest noise droned all around the farm, especially from the forest where owls and bears imported from Earth, and field mice and shrews taken from orbiting habitat sanctuaries, and other non-original animals prowled or fled, alongside prey and predators native to this world.

Club in his left hand, lantern in his right, Sacket strode between the rows of windmills, the long blades slowly turning to grind electricity from the turbines inside the prefab structures. Mice and other creatures scurried away. A tabby-cat mewed at his approach. Ahead, lights across the top of the fence set up to trap the Greenie twinkled.

Laughter penetrated the night noise, blending with the other sounds, including those of the forest, those from the meadow, and those made by the bubbling creek on the far side of the farm.

"It's not the skin," Dora said in a teasing tone-of-voice.

Sacket wondered why they'd stopped at the fence. Why had they come this way at all? The four cottages he kept for visitors were located on the other side of the house, near the stream and the rock-and-thistle garden he'd built to make Jean happy.

Why did Clement and Gibbons come this way?

He dipped into the dark shadow of a windmill, club in hand. He considered the hasty plan that had come to mind. He'd help the Greenie escape the enclosure, and then he'd shoot it, and drag it near enough to the house so this interloper from Prime would know how close they'd been to danger.

A rough plan, he knew. But he'd smooth out the wrinkles. He'd tell Gibbons, "Good thing I decided to walk around the house, for safety's sake, you know."

She'd look confused. Her kind did when confronted with a fait-accompli. She'd look foolish to Clement and Sacket knew his son could never abide a foolish mate. That's why he rejected those giggling farm girls he'd inspected years earlier. It's why he ignored the young women he met at the festivals held to commemorate anniversaries of ship arrivals, and old Earth

77

holidays like World Day and All Peace. When they laughed too much or giggled to one another, Clement frowned.

"It's the eyes," Dora said. "Just like we've got the whites of our eyes, they have green."

Sacket didn't hear Clement's response.

Dora took in an audible breath. "It's for silent communication. Our eyes contrast to the whites and that's how we make non-verbal speech. Same thing for the Greenies."

"How do you know?" Clement asked.

Dora made a sound almost like purring. "My cottage would be more comfortable," she said.

Sacket tightened his grip on the club. He brushed the butt of the pistol at his side, where it sat tight in a rigid holster. He listened to feet scraping a gravel path and peeked out from the edge of the windmill to watch two shadowy figures sway side-by-side.

The sooner the Greenie was destroyed, the sooner Inspector Dora Gibbons would be gone, and then Clement could forget her.

Sacket knelt by a fence post. The electric current running through the fencing set his hair to fluttering. His skin tingled. He lowered his lamp, its light turned down so he wouldn't attract attention. He found where the post met the base, where a clamp held the stanchion in place. A pull on the spring-loaded fastener and a push on the post --

He grunted and struggled with the clamp. When the post popped free, he pushed it aside, enough to make an opening so he could squeeze through with only a mild electric burn along one arm.

The fence surrounded a small section of windmills. He'd have to inspect them all for an intruder, one after the other. He'd have to try each locked door leading to the enclosed turbines. He'd have to walk around the base of each and every unit and look for evidence of a Greenie break-in. He'd need to check each window.

After the first few, Sacket stopped. The fence surrounded six rows of five windmills each: thirty sheds to be checked. Most windows were propped open. Which gave him no choice but to unlock each door, enter the shed, shine his lamp and look into the recesses of the building's interior.

Finding the Greenie could take all night.

"Pop?"

Dora said, "I got an alert." She showed Sacket her communicator and he realized, the break in the fence posts had flipped a virtual switch that gave him away.

"Did you think we wouldn't know?" Clement said.

"I didn't think you'd pay attention. You two being so busy with each other." But he hadn't given the fence and the warning system much thought. Clement was right.

A growl silenced what Clement seemed about to say. A mug-cat pushed its bulk into the space made by the loose fence post. Sparks flew from the wire mesh and the animal howled, its long snout flecked with spit, its incisors bared and its red-on-green eyes flashing. Its short sleek body glistened, shoulders hunched. Sacket respected the animal's power. Its raised head reached waist high and if it stood on its hind legs it was as tall as Clement.

"He's looking for the Greenie," Dora said.

Of course. Which meant, this mug-cat could be used to narrow the search, and that brought a crooked smile to Sacket's face. All they had to do was let this cat prowl from windmill to windmill, sniffing each one in search of its prey.

"Kill it," Dora said. "You've got a pistol. Kill it."

"I need more than this to kill that thing," Sacket hissed. He saw that Clement had his club. Together, they might subdue the cat. Or scare it off. Even wounding it might be enough. Pain would enrage it, but, contrary to myth, it wouldn't attack them if wounded. It would skulk back to its lair to nurse the hurt.

Sacket pushed Dora aside. "Stay back."

She shook him off. "I've never seen one of these up close." She drew a long-nosed pistol with a folding handgrip from her back pocket.

"A tranquilizing dart ain't gonna cut it," Sacket snapped. But it might help. Between their clubs, his pistol, and her dart, they had a chance of fighting this cat to a draw. "Let it find the Greenie for us before you get too wild with that thing."

"Is that all you care about?" Dora said. "Is that why you broke in here? To find that Greenie? And then what? Destroy it?"

Sacket raised his lantern. Clement did the same. The cat sniffed, its knobby black nose bobbing in the air, as though to say, it knew they were close.

A guttural growl exploded from the cat's throat. It rose on two strong hind legs, its dark brown fur rippling in tune to the muscle underneath. Sacket dropped his lantern, drew his pistol, and fired twice. The lightweight weapon bounced in his hand, a burst of sparks surrounding the tip of the long barrel.

Clement stepped up to the cat and clubbed it, striking first its shoulder and then its ribs. A swipe of one claw tore the club from Clement's grip. A second swipe sent Clement reeling with blood spurting from his upper arm. He sprawled on the ground.

Dora aimed her tranquilizer gun. The cat roared. It whined when hit and clawed at its chest. It looked one way, then another, its pointed ears twitching, pink foam at its mouth. Blood trickled from its side. Slowly, head forward, neck stretched, nose close to the ground, it backed up to the fence.

The Greenie sprang from one the windmills, screeching, leaping. It stabbed the cat with a black pointed object in its hand.

Sacket raised his pistol.

"No," Dora screamed.

Sacket felt a sting in his chest. A warm feeling filled his throat. The Greenie leapt from foot to foot.

"You shot him," Clement groaned. "You shot my pop." He struggled to a kneeling position, a hand clamped on his bleeding arm.

The Greenie ran, stumbling and bent over.

Sacket fell to one knee and dropped the pistol. Hands under his arms helped him up, but then he sagged and his vision blurred. He gagged, stomach rumbling. He raked the dirt with his hands, his brain fogged, head aching.

Clement repeated, "You shot him."

"He was going to kill the Greenie."

Sacket fought to push a few words from his dry mouth. "The cat."

Clement stepped towards the fence. Into a pool of blood.

"I used the lowest setting," Dora said, shaking her tranquilizing gun. "I couldn't let you kill the Greenie."

Sacket's throat burned, but his head soon cleared, as did his vision, and he crawled towards Clement, who stooped low where the fence post had been unclamped, near a pool of sticky blood soaking the gritty soil, its red-black surface reflecting the orange-tinged floodlights.

The mug-cat lay on its side, panting, a gash in its neck. Blood streaked the ground, showing where the cat had dragged itself to the middle of the path between two rows of windmills.

Not far off, in a circle of dull light from a tall lamp, the Greenie staggered, and then made another attempt at escaping. Drops of blood scattered across the ground showed that the Greenie had been wounded by the cat.

Dora walked around the dying mug-cat, hands on her hips, head shaking, her stringy hair falling in front of her face.

Sacket grabbed hold of the loose fence post. A stone dagger lay near the mug-cat. He pointed. "The Greenie used that."

Dora mumbled her response. "They're not predators. They don't have the body for it."

Again, Sacket said, "The knife. See?" He let Clement help him past the crackling, sparking fence. The knife on the ground glistened, bloody from use, the natural quartz and polished edges of the stone weapon catching and reflecting whatever faint light fell on it.

"I never realized their weapons were so ..." Dora's voice trailed off. She looked to where the Greenie had been. No sign of it now.

"One of them used its knife on my Jean," Sacket said, remembering the terror in his dead wife's eyes. "I know how they are, how dangerous they can be when cornered, whether you mean to corner them or not."

"Good thing that Greenie was more interested in getting away from the mug-cat than it was in getting away from us," Clement said to Dora. "Else, you'd be lying there with a slashed throat."

Dora picked up the knife. "I want this for the archives. We don't have many of their weapons. Nothing as formidable as this."

"Take it," Clement said, and Sacket detected a catch in his son's voice. He and Dora stood silent and stared at one another for a few seconds. When she walked away, Sacket saw a flicker of regret cross Clement's face.

Loud gasps and shuffling feet broke the quiet. Sacket's other children scurried from behind a row of windmills. They surrounded the dead mug-cat, the two youngest boys crouching for a closer look.

One of Clement's sisters rushed to his side and inspected his wound.

"Where's Inspector Gibbons?" she said.

Clement nodded in the direction that Dora had gone. Then he looked at his father and said, "She had to stop you."

"I could've killed it and been done with it," Sacket said. "Now it'll just come back."

"We don't have to kill them, Pop."

"Look what it did to that cat. That Gibbons woman don't know a thing about our world."

Clement's sister tore a strip of cloth from the hem of her linen nightgown to make a bandage. When she finished, Clement pulled away and walked in the direction Dora Gibbons had taken.

"Where you going?" Sacket called.

"Make sure Dora's okay."

"Leave her be."

Clement loped off into the dark.

"I been killing vermin since I got here," Sacket yelled. "People like her ain't gonna change how we do things."

Clement didn't reply and Sacket stared into the dark, at the after image of the tall young man slipping into the night. There'd be no ordering him back. No use running after him, either.

Sacket blinked. He waved at the dead mug-cat. "Take that thing to the forest," he said, and two of his young sons hurried to do as their father commanded.

Within a Flotsam Web
by WC Roberts

Capture me this feeling above as below
a pale blue dot of heaven

cascading forever through a void,

spider trails of light
blazed in a flotsam web

My anchor thread, my umbilical cord
severed by happy accident,

I am a dream grown outward from
a turning point, maturity

and when children look up in wonder
they'll not see me

with junk, I am discarded

and if nothing can repair this vision
or take me home again,

I'll lift my visor,
the golden mirror shade, my cataracts

that the blinding light of truth
inspire them

and take my breath away

Uhlanga Regio
By Glen R. Stripling

"We're about seven million kilometers from Neptune, Captain."

Captain Oliver Sutherland nonchalantly munched on a strawberry cube as he floated just inches below the ceiling of the *Hornet*. He looked at Lieutenant Baker. "Seven million. We're closer to it than Nereid. We're making good time."

"Yes, Sir. The planet's gravity is pulling us in. We can't stay on autopilot much longer."

Bruce Baker swam right to his commander. "There's something I need to talk to you about. I'm a little concerned about our ship's helmsman. Especially if he's going to be the one landing us on Triton."

"Are you saying Murphy's not qualified?"

"I'm saying something's not right about him. He's been acting real loony."

"Are you talking about last night?"

"You were there, Sir. We had the best beef and vegetable soup Cookie ever fixed and Murphy threw his bottle across the room and screamed, 'I don't eat meat.' He's acting crazy."

Sutherland interlocked his fingers. "This is very odd. Murphy is not a vegetarian. He ate plenty of beef back home."

"It's not that. He's just acting crazy. He's always in a bad mood. He can't pay attention to what he's doing and he always wants to argue with everybody."

"We've been in space for two years now. We all get the jitters every now and then."

"Well I would not want to go down to that moon if he's going to fly with the jitters."

"Alright. I'll keep an eye on him. If I decide he's not fit to fly, I'll fly down to the surface myself."

When Baker went into the forward module, Alice Freemont, the ship's physician, came into the midsection. In her warm gentle voice she said, "Excuse me, Sir. I couldn't help but overhear your conversation with Lieutenant Baker. I'm concerned about Helmsman Murphy too."

Sutherland looked up at her. "Alright. Talk to me."

"Ever since I last examined him, his behavior has gotten more and more erratic. And I am concerned he could be a danger if he is allowed to pilot this ship."

Sutherland brushed his hair. "Professional opinion?"

"Well psychiatry is not my *forte*. But I've observed intense mood swings, agitation and argumentative behavior. And last night I heard him talking in his sleep. He was having some kind of nightmare."

"Did he say anything interesting?"

"He kept yelling, 'Leave me alone. Leave me alone!' He is going through some kind of stress, Sir."

Sutherland nodded. "Alright. I'll talk to him."

*

Peter Murphy "swam" into the central module of the *Hornet*. Sutherland studied his demeanor and saw he was anything but happy.

"Come in Pete. Come over here." They floated about two feet away from each other. Sutherland looked at Murphy. Murphy looked at the floor below him. After a few moments of awkward silence, Sutherland asked, "Pete, has anything been on your mind lately?"

"No, Sir. Nothing in particular."

"You got upset at supper last night because we were having beef. Want to tell me about it?"

"It's just that I don't eat meat. I guess I kind of...overreacted."

"Which explains why you ate a steak the night before we

left Earth."

"I was trying to be polite. The steak made me ill."

Sutherland shrugged. "Murphy, this is the situation. We are billions of miles from Earth. We are on our own. If we screw up this mission, nobody can help us. I need to land a craft on Uhlanga Regio. That's a part of Triton with rugged terrain, ice and snow. You can't make any mistakes landing a craft down there.

"What I need to know is this. If you got a problem that can affect your ability to land a pod down there, I need to know about it now. I'm going to make this a safe mission."

"I'm alright now," Murphy answered calmly. "I've just been thinking about...a lot of things. I can land the pod, Sir."

"Good. Well I suggest you get in the cockpit, get us off autopilot and fly this ship to Triton."

*

Murphy sat in his pilot's seat smoothly handling the controls. He was hoping the crew noticed he had been flying for nine hours and not made a single error.

Dr. Freemont floated up next to him, carrying a sealed bottle of coffee. It was hot but the plastic was thick enough to keep her fingers from being burned. "I've brought you some coffee, Pete," she told him gently.

Murphy took the bottle and noticed a wisp of hot vapor issuing out of the straw. *What?* In the little puff of vapor, he could see the slight glimmer of a face. In a faint voice, it said, "Come join us Pete."

Murphy shoved the bottle back at Freemont. "I don't need any coffee," he growled.

*

Lieutenant Baker looked at the gas giant through his binoculars. Neptune was a big blue silver dollar with three chalk white spiral storms amid the cloud tops. Beside the planet he could see the two rings and their sparkles of light reflecting off the trillions of chunks of gravel. The entire scene was beautiful. It was this he told himself, that made the voyage worthwhile.

When he lowered his binoculars, he noticed Helmsman Murphy floating next to him. Baker handed him the binoculars and told him, "Take a look Murphy. We got three storms on Neptune that are moving at a thousand miles per hour."

Murphy looked through the binoculars at the three pinwheels of clouds. He brought them into sharper focus. And in the pinwheels he could see...faces. And in the slightest whisper, he could hear them say, "We're waiting for you Pete. Come now!"

Murphy handed the binoculars back to Baker and said awkwardly, "That's real nice." Without saying another word, he floated out of the module. Baker was puzzled a moment and resumed looking at the planet.

*

The following day the *Hornet* was in orbit around Triton. Lieutenant Baker floated to his captain and told him, "We started a visual scan of the moon, Sir. We'll be able to record features about half a meter across."

"We'll need it," answered Sutherland as he looked out the window and beheld a world of craters, fissures and ridges. "It's pretty rugged down there and we need to know where every pebble is."

"Are you still thinking of letting Murphy land the *Lassell*?"

Sutherland scratched his lip. "He didn't do too bad at establishing orbit. So far I don't see a really big problem."

"Something I need to tell you, Sir."

"Talk to me."

"During the war, Murphy was a pilot that raided a refinery seized by Islamic extremists. Several civilians were killed in that raid. Rumor has it he's blaming himself for the deaths of innocent people."

Sutherland nodded slightly. "I see." Then he gazed at the wall above him and said dryly, "Well Bruce, as you say, this is all rumor. It's nothing I've observed. I know his behavior has gotten a bit bizarre, but I've seen nothing that makes me doubt he can land the pod."

*

Late that afternoon Helmsman Murphy floated into the aft module of the *Hornet* where he met Sutherland. Sutherland had a global map of Triton on a small computer screen.

"Mr. Murphy, that was a splendid job you did establishing orbit," said Sutherland.

"Thank you, Captain," muttered Murphy.

"Alright, this is what we got," Sutherland began. "We've got a plume of ice and gas on the outer edge of the south polar icecap. We have an active geyser. So what we are going to do is start our descent here at fifteen degrees north latitude, head southeast to sixty degrees south and land just shy of the ice sheet. From there we'll hike through the snow to the geyser.

"We'll take some samples and bring them up here. We'll test them for precious metals and if we find anything we can mine, we'll radio the news back to Earth."

It was then he noticed Murphy was slouching. His face was blank. His eyes were glassy. "Murphy?" he asked. "Are you listening to me?"

"Yes Sir. We'll test for precious metals and if we find anything we can mine, we'll radio the news back to Earth." He answered in monotone.

"Yes but you're not all here. I'm not letting you land the *Lassell*. There's something not right about you." He punched the ship's intercom button and said, "Lieutenant Baker, I need to see you."

"I don't know what's wrong with Murphy," explained Sutherland. "But he is not himself and I can't let him pilot the *Lassell.*"

"I have to say I agree with you, Sir," replied Bruce Baker.

"Yeah. Well now the situation is this. I'm afraid I'm going to have to go down to the surface and pilot the pod myself. There is a possibility I may not make it back up here. If something happens to me, I will need you to command the *Hornet* back home to Earth."

Baker faced the wall below him. He calmly said, "Understood, Sir."

The *Lassell* was a silver egg shaped craft supported by four jointed legs. It had only one engine with a large exhaust nozzle on the underside. The top of the egg was flat with a hatch so the craft could dock with the *Hornet*. It had one side door, which was two meters high.

Sutherland and Dr. Freemont were putting on their spacesuits when Murphy floated up to them. "Captain," he said, "may I be permitted to go down to the surface with you? That is…if you don't feel I will be too much trouble."

Sutherland looked at him calmly. "No you won't be any trouble. In fact we're going to need you to help carry our equipment to the geyser."

"So instead of being your pilot," Murphy said bitterly, "you want me to carry things for you. Like you'd throw a dog a bone."

Sutherland had no time to argue. "No. I want you to do a job that needs to be done. Suit up, Mister."

The *Lassell* was five hundred meters above the surface of Triton. About half way to the horizon, Sutherland could see their target geyser, belching out a tall skinny plume of steamy icy nitrogen.

Dr. Freemont was seated next to Sutherland and advised him, "The geyser is about nine kilometers from here, Sir."

Murphy was seated next to Freemont. "I would recommend landing in the plain to the left of it," he told Sutherland.

"It has a pretty long fissure next to it but I think it will do," the captain answered. Then he added, "Thank you Murphy."

Sutherland flew over a couple of craters on the plain and touched down on a surface of methane ice. For several seconds, the *Lassell* slid across the ice and spun around. It finally came to a stop and Sutherland shut off the engine.

"Is everyone alright?" he asked.

"I'm fine," said Freemont.

"Great," said Murphy.

Sutherland noted his sarcasm. "Murphy," he told him, "I do appreciate your help." Murphy said nothing.

*

They stepped out of the landing pod and climbed onto an icy ground that was bathed by the dim sunlight, which was tinted slightly blue by Neptune's reflection.

They looked at the ice geyser. In the distance they saw it was a misty beam of vapor, lit up by the distant sun. Sutherland felt it was poetic to see the frigid nitrogen gas steam out of the vent at five hundred feet per second into the Tritonian sky.

Murphy's reaction was different. He not only saw the column of gasses. He felt a human presence within it.

When they were about twenty meters from the geyser a thin fog of gasses drifted toward them, as if it were a mild salty breeze on a beach back at home. At that moment the eruption stopped and Murphy could hear a mournful sound that seemed to come out of the geyser along with the nitrogen mist. It was not a sound in his earphones. But it was in his mind. The sound

91

grew louder and became the morbid chorus of human voices. He listened and began to pick up intelligible words.

"Peter. Peter," they said. "We are the souls of the people you killed on Earth. You have been in the world of the living for too long. Now is the time to join us."

"No! No!" shouted Murphy. "Leave me alone."

Dr. Freemont turned to him. "Murphy, are you alright?" she asked.

"Murphy, what's the matter?" asked Sutherland.

"No! No!" Murphy shouted again. "Leave me alone."

"Murphy, what's wrong?" asked Freemont. "Who are you talking to?"

"No! Stop it!" said Murphy. But the voices continued calling his name. He threw down his bag of equipment and sprinted towards the geyser. Using the moon's low gravity, he took giant strides.

"Murphy stop!" shouted Sutherland.

"Peter!" wailed Freemont.

But at that moment he leapt into the geyser.

*

Sutherland knocked on the hard oak door and licked his lips. Moments later an elderly man opened the door and he was joined by his wife.

"Mr. Murphy," Sutherland began, "I'm Captain Oliver Sutherland. I was with your son on Triton when he died."

"Oh do come in," said Mrs. Murphy. "We're so glad you've come to see us."

Her husband did not seem to object, so he followed them inside and they sat down in the living room.

"How did our son die?" asked Mr. Murphy in a laconic tone.

"Well, Mr. Murphy," Sutherland explained, "we noticed your son seemed to be having problems. Something was upsetting him. So out of concern for our safety I did not permit him to pilot our landing pod. But I allowed him to come down to the surface with us. Something made him panic so he jumped into the geyser.

"I wanted to come see you because I feel responsible for us not getting him the help he needed."

Mrs. Murphy answered in a soft voice, "Peter was never the same after the war where he burned all those people in that bombing attack.

"I know he had a big imagination, but he said he was certain he could smell the burning flesh of the people in that fire. He told me it smelled like meat cooking.

"From then on, the sight or smell of anything that had to do with fire would upset him. It didn't matter if it was steaks cooking on a grill, smoke, clouds or fog. Anything like that would drive him crazy. When he saw the vapor coming out of the geyser, he must have snapped."

Sutherland nodded. "Your son was one of the finest pilots who served under me. I was proud to have him with us. And I prefer to believe he is at peace now."

Binaurals
By Josh Brown

"Did you get them?"

Eyrek reached into his pocket and pulled out two small green squares. Each had a series of gold and silver lines running parallel across the top in several directions.

"Right here," he said. "Hot off the press. Serid said they were the most potent he's ever produced."

Zenith was about to plug the green square into the cybernetic implant (cy-plant) located in his wrist; Eyrek stopped him.

"Not here, meteor brain," Eyrek's eyes darted around nervously. "Back in my bunker."

Binaurals were the drugs of the twenty-third century. Chemistry was mostly non-existent on United States Space Station Sector Three, aside from the heavily regulated food-processing department. Food was developed in the susten-lab, and only there, and distributed in the teria on level seven. Plants and all vegetation had become extinct on Sector Three more than 30 years ago.

Electronics, on the other hand, were plentiful, and it didn't take long for the underground to find a way to hack into citizens' cy-plants. At first, binaurals were programmed directly on a citizen's tablet, but tablets were government issued, and therefore subject to tracking. The first binaurals were quickly discovered by Sector Three Surveillance, and hundreds of arrests were made within the hour, causing quite a stir among citizens' rights subcommittees.

Binaurals were a combination of sound frequencies and vibrations, jacked directly into the user's cy-plant. The binaurals directly affected the user's nervous system, affecting his or her physiology, allowing them to obtain a "high" like nothing else.

Each binaural chip lasted only about an hour, and could not be reprogrammed. Most users abandoned their used chip in a garbage chute as soon as it was depleted, wanting to be rid of any evidence as quickly as possible. Any citizen caught in possession of a binaural was proclaimed guilty on the spot and taken directly to lockup.

"Yea," Zenith agreed. "You're right, bro. Let's voom"

He quickly pocketed the chip. Not that they were in any real danger of being caught here, in the back alley of the flea, dull-gray metalcrete and fluorescent light surrounding them. The flea was Sector Three's version of a twenty-first century mall, with people of all manner setting up impromptu tables and kiosks in an attempt to buy, sell, or trade a number of wares, mostly electronics. Fabric and clothes were also popular, but expensive, as they were in short supply on the space station, and much needed due to the heating regulations and the fact that just about everyone had a perpetual feeling of being cold. Space was cold, after all.

Zenith and Eyrek popped out of the back alley and hurriedly navigated their way through the throngs of people amassed in the flea. As they shouldered through the masses, they could hear merchants barking their wares, and more than a few religious fanatics preaching of damnation, salvation, and rapture.

The two boys wanted nothing more than to get back to Eyrek's bunker with their score. These particular binaurals were opiotronics, or "opies" as the kids called them. Effects included sensitivity to sound and light, lowered inhibition, distorted sensory perception, hallucinations, among other things. They were the most popular with kids, who liked to take them alone or in groups, hiding out in their bunkers while they zoned out on their high.

Every citizen had a cy-plant in their wrist, instituted as

mandatory by the government more than one-hundred fifty years ago, surgically implanted at birth. A cy-plant had several functions. First and foremost, it allowed a citizen to be tracked by Sector Three Surveillance at any given time, not that escape was an option on the space station in any case.

A cy-plant also contained a citizen's data records, bank account, and passcodes. Purchases could be made by directly interfacing with a merchant's system, done via the aforementioned 4-mm jack. Same with passcodes—certain citizens had a greater level of access to certain portion of the station, which was verified by interfacing with his or her cy-plant. Each citizen was issued a tablet, an all-inclusive communications and media device, which was accessed via his or her cy-plant.

Each citizen was required to report to Sector Three Surveillance at least once every rotation (two-hundred and seventy seven days, or, one standard station year) and upload their memory. This allowed the government access to every communication, video conference, e-mail, etc. between citizens, as well as access to what books they were reading, what news and net-comm outlets they were accessing, what cines (modern-day equivalent of twenty-first century movies and television) they were watching, and so on.

The method of injection for a binaural was much the same as any other interfacing, except that no trace of its existence could be found after use.

For all intents and purposes, and speaking strictly in terms of pure definition, binaurals were viruses. It got in, ran its program, and got out. A user uploaded a virus into their cy-plant, said virus attacked the user's central nervous system, and the virus then erased itself after the program was complete, essentially covering its tracks.

Eyrek and Zenith hurried through the door as soon as they

arrived to Eyrek's bunker, which was the standard single-citizen fare—six-foot-by-twelve, dull gray and cold metalcrete, and very Spartan.

"Come on, hurry up," Zenith was already jacking into his binaural.

"Dude, what's the hurry?" Eyrek asked.

"I haven't jacked in like a full rotation," Zenith said. "And I don't even remember the last time we've been able to score opies. This is gonna be amp."

Zenith was already plugged in and activating his small green square. Eyrek watched as his eyes rolled back in his head.

"Unnn," was all he said. "Yuh-huh. That's it..."

Eyrek settled down next to his already unconscious friend. He wasn't as impatient as Zenith, who had always been more eager to jack and dose. In fact, Eyrek found himself recently thinking about coming off binaurals completely. Sure, it felt great, but what did he gain, really? In many ways, it was holding him back from doing what he really wanted—finding a cohabitor to get married and applying for a familio license. He could be at the Sector Three familio registration office right now putting his name in the lottery for a cohabitor. Who knows, she might be pretty, or possibly the girl of his dreams. Although government-arranged familios rarely turned out as such. Usually it was a business arrangement, and little more. The concept of "love" was a bit old-fashioned in this day and age.

Eyrek was about to jack when he noticed Zenith begin to twitch. It was subtle at first, but then the convulsions increased, and before long he was shaking so hard that Eyrek was about to put his hands on him to hold him down. Then, suddenly, it stopped. A line of blood began to trickle out of Zenith's right nostril.

"Zenith!" Eyrek slapped his friend, desperately trying to rouse him. "Zenith!" It was no use. He wasn't moving.

97

Freaking, Eyrek ran out the bunker to get some help. The med bay was too far away, so he resolved to run back to the flea to see if anyone could help. But when he got there, his mouth gaped at what he saw, or rather, what he *didn't* see. Nobody was there, not a single person. The flea was totally abandoned. Just mere minutes ago it was a bustling center of activity, hundreds of people, now nothing.

"Hello?" Eyrek called out but the only answer was the echo of his voice.

This isn't right, he thought. *How could this be?* Unsure of what to do, he started off for a security station. Walking hurriedly at first, then breaking into a full-on sprint. Security stations were sometimes manned, sometimes not, but Station 456 near the flea usually had at least one human security official, if only because there was so much activity at the flea.

Eyrek ran through the flea, marveling at its emptiness. The place seemed so much bigger when it wasn't filled with people. He arrived at Station 456, a security station that was little more than a circular kiosk, only to find it empty. Now he was becoming more frightened. He entered the kiosk and stared at the comm array. He had no idea how to use it, so he just started pushing buttons and yelling into a speaker.

"Hello?" he said desperately. "Is anyone there? Where is everyone? My friend needs help!"

Silence.

Eyrek's mind was racing. He had no idea what to do. He again broke into a run, heading back to his bunker. By the time he got back, his chest was heaving and he was gasping for breath. He walked back in only to find Zenith gone.

"Zenith?" he called out. "Z!"

He poked his head back out of the bunker and looked up and down the corridor. It was so quiet he began to tremble.

What is going on? he thought. He collapsed to the floor,

pulling his knees into his chest. Despair washed over him, and he began to sob. He was alone, and the extreme feeling of desolation felt like a hole in his gut. Suddenly, he saw light. He looked up, but saw that the light was not coming from the corridor, or his bunker. It was coming from... him. He marveled as he looked at his hand and saw the faint glow of white light. He held it up and turned it, and noticed that he could see through it; his hand was becoming transparent. He looked down at his chest to see the same phenomenon. He was disappearing.

The glow of white light became more intense, covering his entire body. He felt as if he were going to burst. *Supernova*, he thought. *I'm going supernova?* He felt a squeezing sensation run across his entire body, and cried out in pain. He was on the brink of explosion when he heard a voice. At first it was too faint to make out, but it gradually became clearer. It was his name. Someone was calling his name.

"Eyrek!" the voice called. "Eyrek!" it said again, louder.

Eyrek suddenly felt a jolt. The pain was gone. He was in his bunker, lying on the floor, Zenith frantically shaking him.

"Eyrek!" Zenith said, sounding relieved. "Thank Unisys. I thought you were dead!"

"Huh?" Eyrek propped himself up on his elbows. "What... what's that?"

"After you jacked, man," Zenith said. "You started twitching, then convulsing real bad. You called out my name, then stopped breathing. I slapped you a few times, then I unplugged you, but was worried I was too late. Thought I lost you, bro."

Eyrek sat all the way up. On the ground next to him was a small green square, his binaural.

"Serid wasn't joking," Zenith said. "Potent stuff. One stellar trip, yea?"

"Yea," Eyrek said. "One stellar trip."

Like A Drunken Cosmonaut
By Alan Ira Gordon

Once circled the wide Earth
pioneering lineaged space giants
both astro- and cosmo-nauting

Glenn Godsped
Houston's Eagle landed
Men stepped and mankind leapt

With lofty Sense Of Purpose
collected, measured, tested
the Universe haltingly revealed.

These heirs of Gagarin
aweight with lessened goals and dreams
retreat from striving for the stars

Turn inward as they circle still
with X-Box, Game Boys and the like
a lower case final frontier.

Fathers of Mars
by David Wright

Chapter 1

"Is this your real name?" the beefy port cop barked coldly, and Jas nodded with just the right amount of deference to be completely believable.

It wasn't his real name, not the name his long dead mother had given him. His real name was Chakravarthi Pararajasekarn after his ancient ancestor, King Singai Arya Chakravarthi Pararajasekarn, the original Tamil tiger and forefather of the greatest dynastic clan in the island state of Sri Lanka, perhaps the world. That illustrious name had been shortened by missionary school teachers, immigration officials and 600 years of declining family fortunes down to just three simple syllables, Jas Chakra.

So Jas Chakra he became. But Jas didn't resent the shortening of his name. Marineris Spaceport was a long way from the Sri Lankan royal palace, and when he pushed a mop for ten hours a day for thirty years, it wasn't hard to be humble.

"When did you first hear the gunshots?" This second question from the spaceport cop was asked with equal disinterest as the first. How anyone could be disinterested in the sound of gunshots Jas could only wonder.

Jas had never heard real gunshots before today, or even seen a gun, at least not a real gun. There were no guns on Mars. He'd seen Gun Show clips from Earth. That's what Martians called them anyways, Gun Show clips. Earthers called them by a variety of names--crime dramas, war epics, action-packed, adrenaline-pumping, summer blockbusters. In fact, there were more people killed on Earth Gun Show clips in a year than lived on all of Mars. And Jas, a great lover of Earth Gun Show clips, had witnessed just about every one of those ten thousand deaths.

Needless to say, he knew what gunshots sounded like.

"I'd just finished mopping Gate 97 concourse 4P, so that would make it about 19:30. People were craning their necks like a flock of--"

The port cop looked up from his report, eyes glazing over with boredom. "Cranes?"

"Flamingos." Jas smiled. "But I guess they looked like cranes too. I knew the eight-ball was cock-eyed, so I craned my neck too in the same direction. I saw the flashes in the distance and then I heard the gun shots."

"You saw the flashes from the gun discharge? So you saw the suspect."

Jas nodded, delighted by the port cop's sudden attention. "Saw him clear as a Martian sunrise."

This was no lie. A second after the gun shots echoed off the diamond spaceport walls, a lone figure shot into the air like some mythic hero among mere mortals. No one could stand before him. Port cops were cast aside like children, and those who put up too much resistance were gunned down indiscriminately. Jas should have felt fear, should have ducked beneath his mop bucket and prayed to his mother's ancient Hindu gods for deliverance. But he didn't. Instead he felt nothing but pure exhilaration. He was in the presence of a god.

And then the automatics zapped the intruder with 50 000 volts, dropping him like a rag doll.

"Did he say anything to you? Give you anything?"

Jas looked at the port cop for a long second. "Not a thing, officer."

*

Jas waited a full week before retrieving the little wooden box from its hiding place inside the sewage drain. Porties never checked there because of the smell. Jas had hidden a number of things down the drain before--stun guns, illicit drugs, imprinted data chips--things smugglers wanted buried until the heat was off. They sometimes paid him, sometimes not. But this was the first thing he'd hidden for himself.

When the lightning shot through the Earther, dropping him to the cold tile floor like a rag doll, he didn't die, at least not right away. With a superhuman effort, he got back up. His hands seemed to be fumbling over something, his face straining in pain. He took a few steps, and then fell to his knees in front of Jas.

"Open it," he said, holding out the wooden box in his shaking hands. "Please, op--"

And then he died.

Jas knew he should have turned the box over to the port cops. But he didn't turn it over. On impulse, he dropped it down the sewer grate. And now he couldn't turn it over, at least not without consequences. So instead, he waited for a late shift and smuggled it home under his jacket.

It wasn't much to look at--just a simple wooden box with a bunch of geometric shapes carved into it. Some mass-produced trinket for tourists. Probably wasn't even real wood. But Jas didn't care about the box. Smugglers would use anything to get their stash by the porties. It was what was inside that counted. Only, this box seemed to have no means of opening--no lock, no hinge. He could break it, but then he risked damaging the contents. And what if it was a bomb?

The thought made Jas shudder. He placed the box gingerly on his small kitchen table. Clearly he'd not thought this through. No payoff was worth dying for. In the morning, he would dispose of it, somehow. A dumpster somewhere. Maybe even turn it in--say he found it in the trash. But he wouldn't keep it, not if it meant risking his life.

That night Jas dreamed. This was a rarity in itself. He

almost never dreamed, and when he did, it was usually about the mundane minutia that was the pathetic sum of his waking hours. But this dream was different, fantastical. He saw the great plains of Mars spread out before him, the orange dust rising beneath the marching of ten thousand sons, his sons, a vast dynasty springing up from his loins, and he their great commander, their father, their patriarch, their god.

In the morning, he awoke a different man. He looked at the little puzzle box on his dresser and knew instinctively what he must do. His fingers moved around the box with practiced precision, a stealthy digital dance enacted by some unseen puppeteer, sliding hidden panels on the front and back, twisting corners, notches and along unseen ridges that Jas had not seen before. This went on for some time without Jas ever giving his hands a conscious thought. A dozen combinations, a hundred, a thousand--and then all at once, the box popped open as if driven by a spring.

Jas gazed down in fear and wonder. It had not been a bomb after all. For that he was glad. But it had not been some great treasure either. Slowly he lifted the wooden lid to reveal a small hole just large enough for his finger. This he had seen in his dream so it was no great surprise, but now came the moment of truth, of faith.

The dream had proved true. It had opened the box. But what of the future promises? What of the dynasty he had seen, the great army sweeping across the orange plains of Mars, his destiny? Could it really be this simple, or was it just a dream?

His hand was shaking as he lifted it, no longer possessed by the spirit that had opened the puzzle box. His will was his own again. This would be his decision, his act of choosing without constraint. He saw his ancestors, the great Tamil tigers bowing their knees before him in reverence. He would be the greatest of them all. King Singai Arya Chakravarthi Pararajasekarn would rise again.

With more confidence he slid his calloused index finger into the dark metallic hole. He felt a gentle prick, and then nothing. He frowned.

Chapter 2

Carl Neufeld rushed his very pregnant wife into the hospital.

"Can I get some help here?" he yelled, but no one seemed to pay him any attention. He cast a frantic glance around the crowded emergency room, searching for someone, anyone, in uniform, spotted an orderly, and directed his cries more pointedly in his direction. "Come on, man. Help me! My wife's about to pop. I need a doctor right now!"

The orderly shrugged. "Join the club." And then disappeared behind a curtain.

Join the club? Carl knew Martian health care had been in decline since the war, but this was ridiculous. No, it was criminal. If anything happened to Margaret or his unborn baby, that orderly would lose more than just his job. Carl would make sure of that.

"Carl, he's coming." Margaret squeezed his hand with surprising pressure for such a fair and petite Southern belle. Carl felt his fingers tingle.

"Okay, dear. Just sit here a moment." He lowered his wife onto a molded plastic chair, carefully prying his fingers loose. "I'll get a doctor if I have to drag her in here by her ears."

Margaret gasped. "No time," was all she could manage to say through the pain, and then her water broke.

"Doctor!" Carl screamed in panic, but his voice was immediately echoed by another man screaming the same thing. At first Carl thought he was being mocked, but then he saw the woman next to his wife was also in labor.

And the woman next to her.

And the woman next to her.

If Carl had not been so frantic, he might have wondered about the odds of such a coincidence. As it was, it just gave him enough information to give up on receiving any help from the doctor. He was going to have to deliver his baby, and he was going to have to do it alone.

"It's okay, dear. Lie back. Try to get comfortable. Just breathe." He sounded stupid, even to himself. Margaret gritted her teeth.

"He's coming," she said again, arching her back over the plastic chair. This wasn't how he'd pictured childbirth so many months ago when Margaret came home with the good news that she was pregnant. They knew from the ultrasound that it was a boy. They even named him--Charlie. Wait till they told him how his mother brought him into this world over a plastic chair in the emergency.

Margaret raised her hips even higher, spreading her legs, and Carl saw Charlie's black head crowning. Carl felt his heart jump. So quickly. He was coming so quickly. Carl dropped to his knees and put his hands between his wife's legs, suddenly afraid his baby's head was going to hit the floor like a dropped fly ball.

Margaret screamed as the wet, brown head broke through the birthing canal, and then came the tiny brown shoulders shortly after that. Carl cradled them carefully in his hands, unsure of what to do or say. Margaret was panting heavily, steeling herself for one last push. And then it came.

Carl cradled the little brown baby to his chest carefully. The umbilical cord was still attached and the afterbirth. He wasn't about to mess with that. Margaret was sweating, her head back, eyes closed. He was so proud of her that tears came to his eyes.

He looked down at little Charlie crying in his hands. He was obviously healthy and strong. But there was something odd about him just the same. At first Carl couldn't put his finger on it, but as the adrenalin and passion of the moment began to subside, he saw what it was. Baby Charlie wasn't just dark from the goo and strain of child birth, he was brown--brown as a milk chocolate Easter bunny.

Just as the terrible thought crossed Carl's mind like a noxious cloud of factory smoke in front of the Martian sun, Margaret opened her eyes.

"What is it, Carl? Is the baby okay?"

Carl did not answer.

"Give him to me." Margaret sat up, suddenly worried. She reached out for the baby, and Carl passed him to her. Little Charlie cried, and so did Margaret.

"How could you?" Carl was about to say, but then the man next to him said it first. Carl looked over at him, dumbfounded. The Chinese man had an electro-shock stun gun pointed at his wife and her brown baby. Only then did Carl realize he was a cop.

"How could you betray me like this? Our family? I loved you. I cared for you. I gave you everything." The cop raised the stun gun. It might not kill the little Chinese woman, but it would certainly kill the little brown baby in her arms.

Without thinking, Carl tackled the officer to the ground, knocking over a row of chairs and bewildered patients in the process. There was a brief struggle, but Carl was stronger than the man and less distraught. He wrestled the gun free, and the cop gave up the fight almost immediately, curling up in a ball of self-pity and crying like a baby.

Carl looked back at his wife, who was also crying, and then around the chaotic emergency as if in surreal slow motion. The room was completely filled with new mothers and fathers of every skin color--red and yellow, black and white--but there was only one hue for the newborn babies--milk chocolate brown.

Chapter 3

1086 walked into the Harper's office, is head lowered, a look of grim resentment pasted across his brown face. The head master knew it was 1086 only because the number was printed across the front of his school uniform in large white letters. Otherwise 1086 looked identical to the two thousand other twelve-year-olds at the academy, identical in every way.

Harper checked the roll for the boy's name, found it, and then shook his head in mock disappointment.

"John, there have been reports that you have been fighting with the other grades again. What do you have to say for yourself?"

1086 said nothing.

"John, I don't think you understand how serious this is. The other boy you struck--" Harper searched for his name, but could not find it on the incident report in front of him. It was an older boy from a rich family. That much he knew. His father was on the board, very influential, very dangerous. "He was badly injured. He might have to see a doctor."

1086 did not respond. Harper became agitated.

"His father is threatening to press charges. Do you understand?"

Still nothing. Harper sighed with disgust and sat down heavily in his large leather chair. The boy remained standing and mute.

Behind him, the morning sun cast a red glow across the office furniture, the brown wainscot walls, the academy's many framed awards for excellence in education, and the antique mahogany bookshelf filled with imported volumes from Earth that nobody ever read--ancient encyclopedias, forgotten works of classic literature, massive tomes on archaic religions.

Technically, the books belonged to the Outer-Earth Preservation Society of Mars, but Harper liked to keep them in his office as a status symbol to impress prospective clients. From time to time, he would glance up at their inscrutable spines and wonder about the way things used to be on old Earth. Oh, to have been a man of power back then.

"Look, John, this is your third strike. I'm afraid I have no other choice but to recommend that you be transferred to an adult facility. Is that what you want, John? Look at me when I'm talking to you!" Harper snapped angrily.

He was losing his cool, and he knew it. But there was just something about the twelves that drove him crazy. They acted like they were better than everyone else. Yes, they were stronger and faster and smarter than every other child at the Valles Marineris Academy, winning all the track meets, taking all the top prizes in Math, Science and Literature, but that didn't give them the right to flaunt their superiority. They were just kids, after all.

1086 lifted his head slowly and glared at the head master.

"Well, John, what do you have to say for yourself?" Harper snapped in defiance, not about to back down from the evil eye of any student, not even one as precocious as 1086. And then a more promising threat occurred to him. "What should I tell your father about all this? I'm sure he will not be pleased to hear what you have done. You tell me. What should I tell your father?"

Still nothing, just that glare of pure hatred. And then the boy spoke, biting off each word like it was raw flesh.

"He's not my father."

Harper blinked his surprise at this comment, but before he could respond, the fire alarm rang.

Strange, Harper thought to himself. There was no fire drill scheduled for that afternoon. Could one of the twelves have pulled it? It was a distinct possibility. The twelves stuck together like a pack of wolves. Perhaps they thought it might get their buddy out of hot water. No chance of that.

"This isn't over," Harper scolded.

"Yes, it is. You just don't know it yet."

Harper blinked. "What did you say?"

"His name was Frank, Frank Todd."

Harper was bewildered.

"The boy I struck. The boy whose name you couldn't remember. The Earther boy. It was Frank Todd. And he's not injured. He's dead."

Harper's jaw dropped. He stood up from his leather chair in a rage.

"I've had just about enough out of you, young man. You've bought yourself a month's worth of detentions cleaning the cafeteria. But first you'll write a formal apology to Master Todd's parents. Now get out of my office."

Harper pointed an angry finger at the door, but 1086 just laughed.

"Silly Earther, this isn't your office anymore. It belongs to us. It's not your school either. We saw to that. Hell, it's not even your planet."

"What are you talking about?"

"They're dead. Don't you get it? All the other grades, thirteens, fourteens, fifteens--all dead. As of oh-three-hundred, we killed them all. Teachers too."

Harper took a step back, bumping into his leather chair. He did not believe the boy's story. What head master would? Students would often say things to try and shock their teachers. But he had never encountered such blatant hostility in a student before. Was the boy having a psychotic breakdown?

Harper was about to call in the school nurse, when he heard a scream out in the lobby. He glanced at 1086, who was smirking like the cat who swallowed the canary, and then opened the office door.

Margaret, his secretary of thirty years, was sprawled in her swivel chair, her eyes wide-eyed with wonder at the large red gash in her throat and the fountain of blood that poured out across her frilly white blouse. Around the dying woman in a tight circle, was a pack of twelves with red knives in their hands.

Harper fell back in horror, stumbling over his leather chair and landing with a thud on the hardwood floor.

"What have you done?" he demanded into the copper air, his voice shaking with fear.

"The night of Earthers is over, Head Master Harper. A new day is dawning on Mars, a red day."

1086 walked over to him casually, a large curved knife in his hand.

Chapter 4

Mayor Ruthers huddled in her office, cradling a cup of hot cocoa in her hands and trying not to think about the unbelievable reports that had been blasting across the Martian airwaves all week. Factory bombings. Crashed communications networks. All contact with Earth and other Martian townships cut off. And now invasion?

Mayors were not supposed to deal with such issues. They sat in boring town halls and listened to pencil-necked bean counters drone on about waste management, corporate sponsorship, budget deficits and environmental impact studies. Sure, they glad-handed during elections, kissed babies, made grandiose speeches about change and community spirit, but when it came right down to it, a mayor was just another bureaucrat, another cog in that great universal engine of progress.

They didn't fight wars.

Johnson, the mayor's twenty-something aid and occasional plaything, burst in the door panting like a hyena.

"I thought I told you I was not to be disturbed."

"But they're here." He pointed behind him as if an army was about to step through the mayor's door. His boyish hair flopped over his forehead like a mop and Ruthers wondered how she could have been so foolish to have invited him to her bed. But then, she wasn't the first politician to have made such a mistake. She just hoped her wife didn't find out.

"At the dome airlocks. They're threatening to blow it up and us with it," Johnson continued between gasps.

"Just calm down, Dick. They can't blow it up with combustion charges. The energy dome is impregnable. They can rave all they want out there. Let them drink the Martian sand if they want to, but they won't step one foot in Olympus Mons."

"They don't have combustion charges."

"Ha. Then what are you worried about?" She took a sip of her cocoa calmly even though it was still too hot to drink.

"They have nukes!"

Ruthers felt the cocoa burn the roof of her mouth.

"This message is for Mayor Ruthers. It's time you faced your deepest fears."

The voice was coming from the view screen. Blast it, Ruthers thought. They had taken over the media. What was next? Start chopping off journalists' heads on national TV? The images would circulate for years. How would she ever get re-elected?

"Turn that thing off," she said, taking charge with every microgram of her mayoral authority. "And get me a private line to that terrorist immediately."

"No need for that, mayor," the voice on the view screen said calmly. "I can hear you just fine, and so can the rest of Mars."

Ruthers cringed. He'd bugged her office somehow. He knew everything.

The terrorist was a Chakra clone. That much was obvious from his South Asian good looks and dreamy, saffron eyes. Nobody ever figured out how Jas Chakra, the lowly janitor from the Valles Marineris spaceport, had managed to impregnate more than two thousand women with his clones back in 2197, but ever since then his mysterious offspring had wreaked havoc upon the world of Mars.

They started by taking over a school, slaughtering its students and teachers with psychotic glee. Before anyone knew what had happened, they'd hacked into an airport, a communications tower, a military base, a bank. Their network spread quietly and quickly. High tech security measures were no obstacle to them. They were giants, geniuses in a world of sleeping sheep.

By the time the local security forces figured out what was happening, the Chakra clones had access to every aspect of Martian infrastructure. They opened bridges just as security vehicles were crossing. They ordered government security drones to strike government buildings killing hundreds.

Finally, the military was called in, but by that time it was already too late. The Chakra clones had disappeared, escaped into the vast open territories of Mars, bringing with them enough technology and state secrets to build a worldwide network of terror.

And now, ten years later, they were at her door with a nuclear bomb? Ruthers couldn't believe it.

She would have to be tough with this terrorist, but reasonable. He was probably hungry and tired after ten years in the outback. She could offer him food, perhaps even supplies. But whatever she did, she could not let him inside the dome. It was the only defense left to her.

"What do you want?" Ruthers said coldly, drawing upon her twenty years of mayoral experience.

"From you? Nothing."

Ruthers looked to her aid for an explanation but the pretty young man was speechless with terror. They didn't make men the way they used to. What a shame. She turned back to the terrorist and gritted her teeth.

"Then why are we talking?"

The Chakra clone smiled at her boldness, his dreamy, saffron eyes sparkling with evil humor. "We are talking to you out of common courtesy, a courtesy that was never given to us when we were cruelly institutionalized by this puppet state. Mars, as you know it is about to be destroyed, but a new Mars will rise from its ashes, a true Mars, a pure Mars, a red Mars."

Ruthers did not quake at the young man's rhetoric. She had been hearing this same terrorist propaganda on guerilla bandwidths for nearly a decade. He was just making a show for his deluded followers. In a few minutes, he would open a private channel and beg for some brick rations or algae dishes or solar cells. They were scavengers, pure and simple.

"Thank you for the courtesy," Ruthers goaded. "You are welcome to the rest of Mars, as long as my city is safe."

He raised a sharp, razor-thin eyebrow. "Your city is not the first to be sacrificed. And it will not be the last." He nodded gravely, a strange expression for such a young man.

"What do you mean?" Ruthers felt a chill come over her. This terrorist had a strange way of negotiating.

He stepped away from the camera to reveal a large metal box with a digital timer counting backwards from a hundred.

"What is that?" Ruthers asked, but there was no answer.

The terrorist had apparently left. She turned to her useless aid. The cowardly man looked as if he was about to start crying. "What is it?"

"I told you," he said, angry tears bursting out of his eyes and running down his cheeks. "I told you."

Ruthers kinked her head, and looked back at the view screen. And then it dawned on her.

"Wait!" she called to the walls and ceiling. She stood up, hoping the radio bugs might better pick up the sound of her voice. "Wait. I have supplies. I have money. Whatever you want."

The seconds counted down in mute response.

"I told you," Johnson screamed in terror. "I told you," he said again and then ran out of the mayor's office crying like a little girl who has just lost her puppy.

"I'll let you in," Ruthers said at last. "You don't have to do this. I'll open the shield doors and let you in. Just stop the countdown."

Seconds ticked away.

"Do you hear me? I'll give you whatever you want."

Less than a minute left. Less than half minute.

She was alone now. Her staff had abandoned her, running madly into the street to find their loved ones before the end. But there wasn't enough time. There was never enough time.

She sat down wearily and picked up her cup of cocoa. She took a sip and felt the warmth run down her throat. She cradled the cup in her hands and watched the seconds tick by to oblivion.

Chapter 5

Omari dreamed he was a great warlord chieftain. His Mongol hordes spread out across the vast yellow steppes of Asia as far as the eye could see. No army could stand before him. No woman resist him. He was the supreme ruler of the world. But it was only a dream.

A long time ago, when he was just a small boy, his father told him that he was a direct descendant of the original Khan. Of course, he didn't believe that story anymore. It was just the type of myth that fathers liked to pass on to their children to give them a sense of family pride.

Now that Omari was a father himself, he too wanted what was best for his sons, for their future. And so when he found the gun in the ruins of the burned out city of Olympus Mons, he made a secret pact with himself that no matter how bad things got, he would save the last three bullets for them. He was glad that he was able to keep his promise after all these years. It was important to keep promises, especially the ones you made to yourself.

"Your wife?" Omari asked the question softly, although he already knew the answer.

"Gone. They took all the women. Killed the men. If only..."

"Then you would be dead too."

The fire crackled. Soon it would burn down to the embers and go out. There was no more wood to feed it. They would soon freeze. But no. He wouldn't let that happen.

"I just don't know why they take all the women."

"The Chakra clones are all men. They need our women to reproduce, to give them many children and build their dynasty." There was a time when Omari had hoped to build a dynasty of his own, a humble dynasty in the laundry business, but a dynasty nonetheless.

"It seems so barbaric."

Kuman was Omari's youngest son, strong of arm but soft of heart. Omari could not bear to ask him what had happened to his children, especially his sons.

"Do not despair, my son. We will find your wife. We will find all our wives. And then we will have justice."

Kuman accepted the reassurance without reservation, and Omari felt a pang of guilt. It was a forgivable lie, surely.

Kuman drank the rest of his tea in silence. Omari wanted to give him more, but there was none. Their supplies had run out days ago. The isolation of the polar station had shielded them from the war for a time, but that was of little comfort now. Without food and fuel for the fire, they would soon die.

Omari felt the gun in his pocket. Maybe he should end it now. Why prolong the suffering? But no. There was still time. And if his other sons returned from their journeys, he would need all three of his bullets.

He tucked the heavy pistol deeper into his pocket and attempted to warm his arthritic hands over the dying embers of the fire. A cold gust of wind flooded into the little shelter as the door opened. The embers glowed bright orange for a brief moment, and then died completely.

Rygul entered, frost on his goatee, his cheeks flushed with pink. He closed the door quickly behind him and smacked his arms around his shoulders to beat away the cold. Rygul was Omari's second son. He was a doctor, a surgeon in the state hospital. Omari was proud of his accomplishments, and grieved by his tragedy. His wife and children were some of the first casualties of the war, killed by the bomb that destroyed Olympus Mons City.

"My son!" Omari exclaimed, rising to greet Rygul with a warm embrace. "My heart fills with joy at your return. You made it back."

"Part of me, anyways." He pointed to the frostbite on his nose. He took off his fur mittens and went immediately to the dead fire in a vain attempt to warm his numb fingers.

"And your journey to the hospital? Was it successful? Did

117

you find what you were looking for?"

Rygul stared at the dead embers in silence. Omari felt his legs begin to shake with fatigue and sat down on the old army cot.

"It was some kind of gene splicer technology from Earth. That's all they knew." Rygul spoke without looking up, his blue lips barely moving. "Nobody knows how he got ahold of it. He was just a janitor, for cripes' sake."

Kuman leaned forward, suddenly interested. "What did he do with it?"

"Reproduced his genome a billion times. Sent it out into the atmosphere in microscopic spores that found their way into every ovulating female within a hundred-mile radius. Talk about your horny toads." He laughed bitterly.

Omari's own wife had been one of those ovulating females thirty-two years ago. When the little brown baby came out of her womb, he thought his wife had been unfaithful. He considered divorce, even murder. But then when he saw that the same thing had happened to two thousand other women, he thought it was a miracle. How could he have known that those miracle children would one day destroy his entire world?

"But what about Earth? What about the military? There must be something we can do to stop them," Kumar raged excitedly, until Rygul turned on him.

"There's nothing we can do!" he snapped. "Nothing Earth can do. Mars Com satellite received a message from them just before it went off-line. Bio-bombs have ravaged the planet, wiped out crops, cut the population in half. They're in shambles. And as for Mars military, they were routed at Schiaparelli Crater. The war is lost. The only thing left is extermination."

"I don't believe that," Kumar whined in defiance of his older brother. "Morgus said he found a weapon. He'll fight them.

You'll see."

Rygul sneered, but his rage had left him. He was done fighting. He put his hands back over the dead fire and fell silent. Omari fondled the weapon in his pocket. The time was approaching, but not yet. Not yet.

It was nearly morning by the time Omari's oldest son arrived. Morgus had always been the pride of his life, the strongest of his children and the wisest. But Omari held out no vain hope that he had found any kind of weapon that could help them. The Chakras had the cities. They had nukes. Nothing could help them now.

"I found it, father," he said, his mad eyes glowing silver with excitement. "It was hidden in the sewers of the old spaceport. Nobody would look for it there. Nobody but me."

It must have been the cold that had taken his mind, or the loss of his family. Omari would have cried if he wasn't so tired. He felt the weight of the gun in his pocket and knew that the time for its use was rapidly approaching. He just hoped he could kill them all with a single shot each. He could not bear it if they were simply wounded and forced to endure a long and painful death.

"What is it?" Kuman exclaimed, nearly falling out of his chair. "Let me see."

"No," Morgus snapped, wrenching the bundle out of his brother's reach. "This is for father." He placed the bundle onto the table next to the dead fire and began to unwrap it slowly, one fur at a time. When he was done, nothing remained but a small wooden box.

"Is this your weapon?" Rygul laughed harshly, but Kuman shushed him.

"How do you open it? What's inside?" he reached for it again, but Morgus held him at bay.

"I know how to use it. Look." He ran his fingers deftly

across the intricate designs on each side of the box. With a strange shuffling sound, the box came to life and opened to reveal an oval mark just barely visible in the candlelight.

"Touch it, father."

"Why? What will it do?"

"It will multiply your offspring a thousand times, a million times, more than all the stars in the night sky. The Khan dynasty will rule Mars. It will live on forever."

Omari gazed into the weary faces of his three sons, each in turn. They would grasp at any hope, no matter how foolish. He felt the gun in his pocket. Wouldn't it be better just to end it all now?

"How do you know this?" he said at last.

Morgus smiled. "I had a dream."

Omari was surprised by that answer. He too had had a dream, a dream of a great dynasty that swept the world. He gazed down at the simple box for a long moment. Could this really give it to him--his heart's deepest desire? He fondled the gun in his pocket one last time and reached for the box.

A Star-Struck Night
By Robert P. Hansen

The grass is chill beneath my back—
a contrast with the warm June breeze—
as I lay staring at the sky
with starlight's glimmer through the haze

of smog. The city lights obscure
their brilliant astronomic gleam,
but they're up there, small twinkles where
the atmosphere distorts their dream-

like wonder. I am here, adrift,
alone, amid a tangled throng
of aliens, with fertile earth
beneath my back. But not for long.

One star I cannot see is mine,
but soon the ship will come for me,
and when I leave, I'll leave behind
a world enthralled in slavery.

Earth Camp
By Alicia Cole

The scholarship notice crumpled in San Helfjord's hands.

"Second best," he grumbled. His acceptance to Andar Prime's Flight Academy had come without money attached.

After the past three seasons' poor yield, the family had little extra.

*

Earth Camp. Light years from home.

"I've never even left the moon's orbit," Gaer Fain, seated a row behind San, said.

"Jump check," the captain announced over the com.

San bit down on the air tube in his mouth, as a flight cadet checked the seal.

"You need to put your breather in, cadet," Halcyon Tol, a Revlokian Corporal, admonished Gaer.

Tol's large, cracked, and reddened hands, tri-fingered, secured Gaer's sealant.

"Front and center, soldier. Keep your head."

"Ten...nine...eight..."

San breathed, remembering his mother's face as she helped him pack his bag.

"Seven...six...five..."

San breathed, remembering his father's hands clasping his own.

"Four...three...two..."

San breathed, remembering his girlfriend's parting kiss.

"One."

The hull of the ship seemed to dematerialize around him.

San's head felt light, then felt as though it had been placed under his feet, then felt nothing at all.

"Cadet got sick," Halcyon Tol reported to the Captain, a slim man of Terran build.

Gaer doubled over on the dry ground, heaving.

A burlier cadet, head shaved, sneered.

"Give him a chew," came the order.

"You," the burly cadet was addressed, "Help with the equipment."

"You and you also."

San and a female cadet stepped forward.

Her hair was piled in a bun, and the sun glinted ochre on the strands.

The grey earth around them lifted in dry bursts as the air gusted.

*

"You should try the chews sometime," Gaer said, a wry smile on his lips. "They take the pale right out of you."

The small group clustered around the fire, heavy bags piled close.

San lay back and watched the stars.

"More animal life has returned, sir," Laira announced, returning to the corona of the campfire's light.

"Mostly invertebrate arthropods, though I saw something small and furry. Could have been a rodent."

"Rabbit, most likely," Halcyon said.

Laira made a fast addition on her wrist-pad, tallying the list of organisms seen.

"And the scrub?"

The Captain was making his own notes.

"Creasote and ambrosia are plentiful."

"Excellent! I hadn't expected that much growth since our last visit."

Halcyon's hands turned a bit of earth between long,

cylindrical fingers. "Hardy planet."

"Thankfully."

*

The desert flushed hot with the morning sun. The cadets covered their heads with tinted, breathable fabric.

It was a long walk to the bio-dome, intentionally so. Even the faintest back-fumes from a ship could unsettle the delicate environmental balance.

"Do you wish you'd gone to the Flight Academy?" Laira asked, breathing hard as they trudged across the sand.

"Instead of counting creosote bush?" San smiled wryly and readjusted his pack, huffing. "Nah, my...girlfriend would love the yellow flowers."

"Ah," came Laira's disappointed reply.

San chose not to look at her.

*

The dome, silver and solar-paneled, cast a heavy shade on the surrounding land.

Inside, the air was moist.

San heard birds in the canopy of the arboreal forest as he entered his assigned domain.

"Better than shooting down Fahrlings?" Halcyon Tol placed a heavy hand on San's shoulder.

"Yes, sir," he said, bending to cup his hand over a fern. The leaves flushed together.

"I prefer the free ride to re-growth."

Some Things Come Unbidden
By Lisa Timpf

Through a mist of tears
she admires her
grandson s tiny, perfect, grasping
fist
making a cradle of her arms she
rocks him
singing a snatch
of a half-forgotten lullaby
rife with bland, innocent imagery
not the stuff of nightmares, surely
something her own mother taught her
half a galaxy away
the way things are handed down
through generations
she knows, now,
that some things come unbidden
though from this angle
you can't really see
what is sprouting
from the newborn's back
besides, she should be happy,
she tells herself
to know that her descendants
will fly
someday.

The Tulku of Titan
By Mike Morgan

"The ashes blew straight up," repeated Sonam quietly, "as if they were caught in a vortex. There is no clearer sign than that."

The wind was whispering softly as the committee of High Lamas meditated on the shores of the lake. Sonam should have been relaxing into that meditation along with the rest of the committee, but his thoughts were restless, colored with anxiety. No, it was more than anxiety: it was dread.

"Yes," replied Yonten sadly, sitting cross-legged to his left and equally failing to meditate. "It was only a matter of time."

"And the Oracle couldn't get any clear sense of him here on Earth," Sonam continued, the words slipping from the corner of his mouth.

From his position in front of them, Saragarhi turned his head and regarded the pair sourly, all meditative quiescence gone. "Your minds seem scattered today, brothers. But you may calm yourselves. I have had the vision that we seek."

Sonam asked in surprise, "You have? Already?"

Saragarhi nodded. Gently, he added, "Tell me Sonam, do you enjoy long journeys?"

"You know I do not," answered the lama.

Saragarhi let out a sigh. "Then I fear you will not like what I saw."

Sonam felt the dread settle about his shoulders, bearing down on him like a dead weight. "Is the tulku we seek so very far away?"

Yonten muttered crossly, "You know how contrary Gendun Gyatso could be. He even said before he died that he'd use his phowa as a way of protesting what's happening here in Nepal."

Sonam ignored Yonten and stared beseechingly at Saragarhi. "Tell me," he pleaded.

126

The older lama replied serenely, "My vision was of an orange moon orbiting Saturn."

"No," exhaled Sonam, before he could stop himself.

Saragarhi continued, "And of a small metal thing that floated near it. The metal place looked very old, almost worn out, I'd say."

"Getting there is going to cost a packet," spat Sonam.

Saragarhi had the cheek to simply shrug in response to the financial objection. "We must go where we must. The days when we searched only in the local region are long gone."

Yonten interjected diplomatically. "I'll get some pictures of the moons of Saturn. Let's see if our brother can identify which one he saw in his vision." He smiled beatifically. "Once we have the moon pinned down, it should be relatively straightforward to establish what station we need to visit."

The lama stood up slowly, his aged joints stiff. "Don't fret, Sonam. I'm sure the flight won't last more than a year. Eighteen months, tops."

*

Molly Douglas was trying to get Oli to nap when Commander Hanover called. With her three-year-old child shrieking in the background, she answered the line.

"Molly? Sorry to disturb you, but something rather important has come up." She found she couldn't quite tell what expression was on Hanover's face in the small image projected by the wall-mounted communicator. He looked as amused as he was panicked, the two conflicting feelings warring for territory on his features.

"Is there an issue with a flight plan?" she asked, confused. "I'm off shift right now, but I suppose I can come in if you need me in Control. I'll have to get hold of Maureen to watch Oli for a while, but--"

"No, it's nothing to do with work," interrupted Hanover.

"All the traffic you were tracking prior to end of shift is fine."
He paused, "Actually, the inbound cargo transporter docked
already. The, ah, people who want to see you were on it."

"People?" she queried, changing mental gears rapidly.

"Yes. Well, I say people, but 'delegation' might be a better
term for them." He smiled nervously. "You don't mind if they
drop by, do you? I'll pop along with them, just so you know
there's nothing fishy going on."

Molly didn't know what to say. "Oli is meant to be taking a
nap," she began, but then she realized the station commander
was going to arrive in her cabin in just a few minutes and the
cramped confines of her living quarters were a cluttered, toy-
strewn mess.

"We won't keep you for long," replied Hanover, bulldozing
his way through her feeble argument. "And they've come a long
way to see Oli."

"Oli?' squeaked Molly in disbelief, but Hanover had already
hung up.

*

Molly made tea for the Buddhist lamas. It seemed like the
right thing to do; although, on reflection, it was probably the
wrong type of tea.

Twenty minutes notice had barely been enough time to
shove toys into the under-bed storage bins and straighten the
sheets. There was still a pile of dirty dishes in the tiny galley's
sink.

There were three men in the Buddhist delegation; each one
was stooped and wiry, dressed in robes of dark crimson and
golden yellow, with tall hats shaped like rooster combs. The
color of their hats and under-robes wasn't entirely dissimilar to
the light orange atmosphere of the moon the station was
orbiting.

They introduced themselves, in faltering Standard, as

Sonam, Yonten, and Saragarhi. Apparently, there should have been more than three of them--there should have been an entire committee and a gaggle of officials--but space travel was enormously expensive and they'd been forced to economize.

Given the limited amount of space available in her single-room cabin, the three lamas were perched on the edge of Molly's bed while the commander occupied one of the bar stools at the breakfast counter. Oli was racing around, bouncing off people's legs and reveling in the opportunity not to nap.

While she waited for the kettle to boil, Molly attempted conversation. "We don't see many outfits like those on Titanville. You sure won't be hard to miss while you're staying here. What do you call those? Robes?" They were sure different from Oli's plain unisex coveralls and Molly's lightweight pants and tunic.

"Yes," answered the one who'd introduced himself as Yonten.

The middle lama, who looked a little younger, muttered something disgustedly about not having ceremonial clothes with them on account of not being able to afford the increased luggage weight.

Yonten made a tiny gesture and the other Buddhist clammed up; strangely, they had an air of naughty schoolboys trying to be on their best behavior. They were also clearly very interested in Oli.

The oldest of the lamas asked Hanover with a piercing glare, "And you're sure no other child was born on the date we specified?"

Hanover shrugged. "Titanville has a population of exactly four thousand six hundred and twelve permanent residents, and since we're all cooped up in the same tin can, it's kind of easy to keep track. So, yeah, I can say with absolute authority that you're looking at precisely the only kid born on August fifteenth or on any day near then: little Oli Douglas."

The lamas went back to staring at Oli. The kettle boiled loudly.

*

"You think Oli might be the Dalai Lama," repeated Molly stridently.

She nearly poured the hot tea right over the elderly Buddhist, but steadied her aim just in time. The second his cup was full, she put the pot back down on the counter, not trusting herself with it anymore.

"The Dalai Lama is a type of bodhisattva called a tulku. He is able to reincarnate by choice. During his phowa, his transfer of consciousness, he can decide how he is to reincarnate. This time, we think he may have chosen here," explained Yonten.

Molly struggled to recall the details of the Dalai Lama's passing. Titanville was a long way out, but the Earth news still reached them even if it did arrive a few weeks late. "Didn't he die, what, three years back or thereabouts?"

"Yes," said Sonam heavily. "That's right."

She got the point; Oli's birth coincided with the Dalai Lama's passing. "This is ridiculous," she protested. "We're not Buddhists. And Titanville is a shabby, forty-year-old hydrocarbon processing plant left over from the start of the twenty-third century. Everything here has seen better days. Your leader isn't going to want to be born into any place like this."

Hanover interrupted, "They have a test they want to perform. It won't hurt Oli. They already talked me through what they want to do, and there's nothing dangerous involved. Can they go ahead?"

Molly pursed her lips. "If you think it's fine, I guess so. They have come all the way from Tibet."

The most wrinkled of all the lamas, Saragarhi, corrected her

130

as he pulled a small bundle out from the folds of his robe. "We had to leave Tibet over two centuries ago. These days we are based in Nepal, but I think our association with that country might be coming to an end soon too. The country is a dictatorship and the government is interfering in our religion just as the Chinese did in Tibet."

Saragarhi finished unwrapping the bundle. In the open folds of the material, six small items were revealed. Molly could see some keys, a necklace, a statue of a bird, and some other jewelry. They looked like personal effects.

The lama called softly to Oli to come take a look. Oli hesitantly tiptoed over and peered at the objects.

Sonam said quietly, "Oli, two of these things are yours. Can you pick them out? We'd like to give them back to you."

The child's hands flashed, and before Molly could blink, the key and the tiny bird statue were gone from the collection of items.

"That's right," said Yonten. "Thank you, Gyatso."

*

"So what's next? Oli's the head of a major religion, all of a sudden?" sighed Molly, wishing she had something strong to slip into her tea.

"Next, the child will be shown to three associates of the Dalai Lama to confirm his identity," announced Saragarhi. "The selection of the correct personal items was merely a first step."

Molly's eyes almost popped out of their sockets. "Now you just hold on there, pal. Oli's not going anywhere! Certainly not Earth!"

Sonam's mouth fell open. "But the Dalai Lama must be trained in a monastery. He has to go to Nepal--"

Yonten abruptly said, "Are you sure? We're about to be forced out of there. Perhaps it is not wise to bring the reincarnated Dalai Lama into such a dangerous situation."

Saragarhi considered the point, eventually replying, "Many of our teachings are spread through electronic communications nowadays. It's not inconceivable that a Dalai Lama could be trained off-Earth and spend much of his time out here. He would still have the same impact on followers throughout the Solar System."

He peered at Oli, adding, "With so many people leaving Earth and moving to the Outer Worlds, is that what you intended? That we should look to the future, and move somewhere we will not be oppressed?"

Oli said, "I like ice cream and penguins!"

Molly raised a hand to get their attention. "Excuse me, but you've said 'he' a couple of times now. I think there's been a bit of a misunderstanding."

Saragarhi shook his head, bemused. "There is no misunderstanding. Oli is short for Oliver, is it not?"

Molly winced. "It is sometimes. In this case, it's short for Olivia."

Sonam started laughing, and it wasn't long before Yonten and Saragarhi joined in. "That removes any lingering doubt," gasped the youngest of the three lamas. "Being in space wasn't enough for Gendun Gyatso; naturally, he would only settle for also reincarnating as the first female Dalai Lama."

He wiped tears from his eyes and stood up from the bed. "Miss Douglas, we'll see you bright and early in the morning. Olivia will be a good student, I hope."

Biographies

Josh Brown:

Josh Brown is the creator of *Shamrock*, a fantasy-adventure comic that appears regularly in *Fantasy Scroll Magazine*. His poetry has appeared in *Abandoned Towers Magazine*, *Pixies of Eglantine*, and *Poetry Quarterly*. His short fiction has appeared in anthologies from Sky Warrior Books, JWK Fiction, and Hydra Publications. His comic work has appeared anthologies from publishers such as Desperado Publishing (*Negative Burn*), Alterna (*Alterna Tales*), and more. He currently lives in Minneapolis with his wife and two sons.

David Castlewitz:

After a long and successful career as a software developer and technical architect, David has turned to a first love: SF, fantasy, and magical realism. He's published stories in Weirdyear, Farther Stars Than These, Fast Forward Festival, Encounters and other online as well as print magazines. Visit his web site: http://www.davidsjournal.com to learn more and for links to his Kindle books on Amazon.

Alicia Cole:

Alicia Cole lives with a photographer and a menagerie of animals in a house backed by woods. They have many alien visitors to their property. No real aliens, unfortunately, though there's landing space at the nearby airport where her husband flies. Her work is forthcoming in Torn Pages Anthology and Steel Cities.

T. Fox Dunham:

T. Fox Dunham lives in Philadelphia with his wife, Allison. He's a cancer survivor, modern bard and historian. His first book, The Street Martyr, was published by Gutter Books. A major motion picture based on the book is being produced by Throughline Films. Blood Bound Books is publishing his second book, Mercy, a horror novel based on the torture of his cancer treatment. He has a story to be included in the second Stargate anthology, Far Horizons. Fox is an active member of the Horror Writers Association, and he's had published hundreds of short stories and articles. His motto is wrecking civilization one story at a time. Site: www.tfoxdunham.com. Blog: http://tfoxdunham.blogspot.com/. http://www.facebook.com/tfoxdunham & Twitter: @TFoxDunham

Alexandra Erin:

Alexandra Erin is a speculative poet and author best known for the self-published web serial Tales of MU. Her poetry has appeared in the pages of Stone Telling, Devilfish Review, and Star*Line.

Alan Ira Gordon:

Alan Ira Gordon has published in both genre and mainstream short story and poetry markets. His fiction appearances include Starshore Magazine, Disturbed Digest and Worcester Magazine, and he's a regular contributor to the Whortleberry Press "Strange Mysteries" anthology series. Gordon's poetry has been featured in The Magazine of Fantasy & Science Fiction, Analog, Beyond Centauri and FrostFire Worlds, and he's a frequent contributor to Star*Line, the journal of the Science Fiction Poetry Association (SFPA). Further information on his publications is available on his website at www.alaniragordon.com.

Robert P. Hansen:

Mr. Hansen teaches philosophy courses at a community college and has just finished the fourth book of his Angus the Mage fantasy series. His novels and collections (stories and poetry) are available in eBook and print form. Visit his blog (http://rphansenauthorpoet.wordpress.com/) for descriptions, reviews, and links to online retailers.

David C. Kopaska-Merkel:

David C. Kopaska-Merkel has edited Dreams & Nightmares since the 80s. Since the 70s his poetry, fiction, & reviews have been published in scores of venues, including Asimov's and Strange Horizons.

Andrew MacDonald:

Andrew L MacDonald writes from Ottawa, Canada. A mechanical engineer by day, he spends every other moment transcribing his daydreams of traveling the solar system that all started with a university spacecraft systems design course.

Mike Morgan:

Mike was born in Hounslow, London, but moved to Stoke-on-Trent when he was 18. At 30, he realised accountancy wasn't the exciting life he'd anticipated and relocated to Japan. After falling in love with an American, Mike relocated to Houston, Texas. These days, Mike lives in Iowa with that American lass, who is now his wife, as well as two young kids. He hopes that he will never again have to move between or across continents.

Most recently, Mike has written for Uffda Press for their King of Ages anthology, Flame Tree Publishing for their Science Fiction Short Story anthology and Pole-to-Pole Publishing for their Hides the Dark Tower anthology. But he's also been a contributor to various volumes on Doctor Who, including You and Who 1-3, Shooty Dog Thing 2, Shelf Life, and Drabble

Who. Lately, he's taken up writing about Blake's 7, with an essay in You and Who Else.

He's also written a comic strip for the small press comic, Futurequake, and he's currently a regular contributor to the website WhatCulture.com, with over 1.5 million views to his name. But the work he's most proud of getting into print was the purely-for-the-love-of-it cartoon series "Frank the Macra" in the well-regarded and now sadly defunct Doctor Who fanzine, Shooty Dog Thing. You can find it on his Tumblr blog at CultTVMike.

WC Roberts:

WC Roberts lives in a mobile home up on Bixby Hill, on land that was once the county dump. The only window looks out on a ragged scarecrow standing in a field of straw and dressed in WC's own discarded clothes. WC dreams of the desert, of finally getting his first television set, and of ravens. Above all, he writes, and has had poetry published in *Strange Horizons, Apex, Space & Time Magazine, The Martian Wave, Aoife's Kiss, Scifaikuest, Star*Line*, and others.

Jerry L. Robinette:

Jerry L. Robinette is an Operations Expert with a major health insurance company in Central Ohio. He is a graduate of Clarion (at Michigan State), The Oregon Coast Writers Workshop, and the Ohio State University.

EJ Shumak:

Mr. Shumak lives in metro Chicago, Illinois, and has spent most of his life in northern Illinois and southern Wisconsin. He has been many things, police officer, large cat sanctuary operator, C.P.A. and on again, off again writer. Lately on again. He has held active membership in S.F.W.A. since 1992, and has sold four books, three fantasy novels and one non-fiction along with several dozen short science fiction pieces and non-fiction articles. Some of his current work is available at amazon.com/authors/ejshumak

Christina Sng:

Christina Sng is a speculative poet, writer, and occasional toymaker. She is a two-time Rhysling nominee and her poetry has received several Honorable Mentions in the Year's Best Fantasy and Horror. In her free time, she plays the ukulele, dreams of exploring the Andromeda Galaxy, and carves out new worlds in longhand, imbibing an aromatic cup of tea.

Matthew Spence:

Matthew Spence was born in Cleveland, Ohio and lives in Parkersburg, West Virginia. His work has appeared in Under the Bead, New Realm, Nebula Rift, and EGM Shorts.

Glen R. Stripling:

Glen Stripling is a sci-fi writer that has published in various magazines, including SHELTER OF DAYLIGHT, OXFORD SO AND SO, and A ROBOT, A CYBORG AND A MARTIAN WALK INTO A SPACE BAR. He published his first novel CHRONOSIA in 2008. He now lives with his wife Katherine in Lake Lorman, Mississippi.

Lisa Timpf:

Lisa Timpf is a freelance writer who lives in Mulmur, Ontario, Canada. Her writing has appeared in a number of venues, including *Chicken Soup for the Soul: Christmas in Canada, Morel Magazine, The Heron's Nest, Imaginate*, and *On the Premises.*

David Wright:

David is a writer and English teacher living on Canada's majestic west coast. He has a lovely wife, two sparkling daughters and fifty published short stories. His work has appeared in dozens of magazines including Neo-opsis, Aphelion and Silverthought. He currently has three novels available at Amazon Kindle and Smashwords.

Seedlings on the Solar Winds by J Alan Erwine

America as a fascist state, soldiers driven to terrorism, insane computers, insane humans, insane aliens, these are just some of the things waiting for readers in the pages of this new collection from prize winning science fiction author J Alan Erwine.

Seedlings on the Solar Winds contains sixteen stories that will have readers question what reality really is, and wondering what the future of humanity might be.

"J Alan Erwine is a master at placing believable characters into plausible, and often dark, futures. In the process, he unflinchingly explores what is both base and noble about humanity." – David Lee Summers, editor Tales of the Talisman and author of Heirs of the New Earth.

"...Erwine always presents a banquet of plots and characters [not all of them human], generously seasoned with pith. You can relish him as the main course in your reading, or save him for dessert..." – Tyree Campbell, author of Nyx and The Dog at the Foot of the Bed.

Order from our bookstore at:
http://nomadicdeliriumpress.com/blog/product/seedlings-on-the-solar-winds/

Order the e-book at:
https://www.smashwords.com/books/view/16551

The Fifth Di...

The Fifth Di... is a science fiction and fantasy magazine that was first published by ProMart Writing Lab as a print zine. Eventually it was moved to the web, and then with the passing of ProMart founder Jim Baker, Tyree Campbell took the little webzine with him to Sam's Dot Publishing. Along with the zine, Tyree also brought along the zine's editor, J Alan Erwine, and now that J has left Sam's Dot, he's brought Jim's little magazine to Nomadic Delirium Press.

In its new format, The Fifth Di... will be an inexpensive quarterly webzine that will be downloadable for just $2.00 from Smashwords, and other retailers...and yes, it will be available for both the Nook and the Kindle.

Visit The Fifth Di...:
http://nomadicdeliriumpress.com/fifth.htm

The Ephemeris Science Fiction Role Playing Game Created by J Alan Erwine & Joshua Kviz

The year is 2185. The human race has gone to the stars, and found that they're not alone. Local space is teeming with civilizations, some hostile, some friendly, and some indifferent. This is the universe of Ephemeris.

Ephemeris is a game of galactic trade and galactic conquest; of inter-species conflict and cooperation. Ephemeris is a science fiction role playing game. Here you will be able to take on the role of your favorite alien species and your favorite class. You will be able to trade, fight, negotiate, conquer, whatever you'd like to do with your fellow players. You can play the role of an Althani Trader, or maybe an Arbonix Cyber Wizard, or maybe even a Human Nanist. You can create a party made up entirely of one species and set out to upset the trade routes of a rival species. Or maybe you want to create a party with a variety of races that preys upon the trading routes of the various civilizations. Or maybe you want to explore the ancient ruins on long dead planets, ruins that clearly show that there were other species roaming the spaceways in the past...but where are they now? You can fight in great wars, negotiate grand peace treaties, and explore sections of the galaxy that no sentient has ever explored. Or maybe your party has joined with one of the interplanetary corporations; corporations whose motives are never entirely clear.

These are just some of the possibilities open to you. The universe of Ephemeris is yours to do with as you please. What you now hold in your hands are the basic guidelines for the games. Here you'll find the races, classes, abilities, skills, weapons, and ships that allow you to create your own Ephemeris universe.

Now, step inside for the greatest science fiction adventure you've ever been on...

Order from us at:
http://nomadicdeliriumpress.com/blog/product/ephemeris-a-science-fiction-rpg/

Order from DriveThruRPG at:
http://rpg.drivethrustuff.com/product/63664/Ephemeris

Check out all of the Nomadic Delirium Press titles at:
http://nomadicdeliriumpress.com/blog/shop

You can find Nomadic Delirium Press e-books at:
https://www.smashwords.com/profile/view/nomadicdelirium

Feel free to comment on any of the stories or poems in this issue by visiting our blog:
http://nomadicdelirium.wordpress.com/

www.ingramcontent.com/pod-product-compliance
Lightning Source LLC
Chambersburg PA
CBHW070750120626
46557CB00002B/527